SILVER SPOON UNDERWORLD

Belle's KING

USA TODAY BESTSELLING AUTHOR
LONI REE

BELLE'S KING

Copyright © 2023 by Loni Ree

All rights reserved. No part of this book may be reproduced in any form or by any electronic or mechanical means, including information storage and retrieval systems, without written permission from the author, except for the use of brief quotations in a book review.

Please respect the author and do not participate in or encourage piracy of copyrighted materials that would violate the author's rights.

This is a work of fiction. Names, characters, businesses, places, events, locales, and incidents are either the products of the author's imagination or used in a fictitious manner. Any resemblance to actual persons, living or dead, or actual events is purely coincidental.

Edited By: Kendra's Editing and Book Services

Cover Design By: Cormar Covers

Cover Photography: Xram Ragde

Created with Vellum

SILVER SPOON FALLS UNIVERSE

We're taking over the universe. 🤭 JUST KIDDING!

Nichole Rose and I are actually building our own little world-the Silver Spoon Falls Universe. Welcome to the Silver Spoon Falls Universe, where forever means exactly that.

We hope you'll join us this year and next as we introduce you guys to even more of the men and women who call Silver Spoon Falls home in the Silver Spoon Falls series, the Silver Spoon Underworld series and the Silver Spoon Falcons series.

Don't worry! We will continue writing our own books too! And these will connect in new and exciting ways to our own worlds, creating one giant book universe for you to explore!

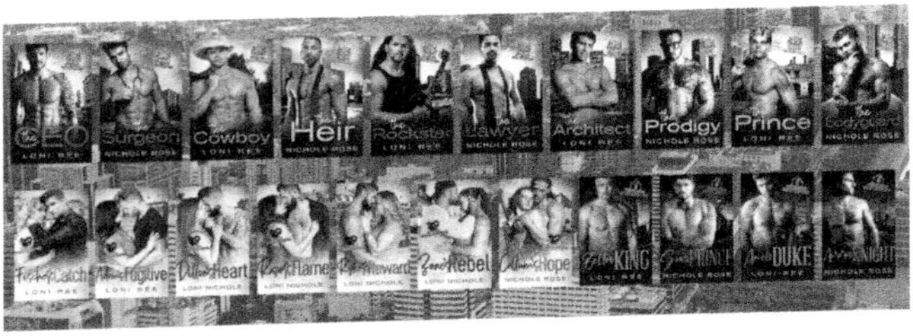
Surgeon
Cowboy
Heir
Lawyer
Architect
Prodigy
Prince

SILVER SPOON FALLS

Welcome to Silver Spoon Falls, TX. The men here are known for having it all. Except there's a shortage of eligible ladies in town to share it with. These determined men won't let that slow them down. Like the MC brotherhood who calls this small-town home, their best friends, brothers, and neighbors will turn the town on its ear looking for their curvy soulmates in this spin-off series of sweet and steamy instalove romances from Loni Ree, Nichole Rose and Loni Nichole.

You've already fallen for the Silver Spoon MC. Now get ready to fall for the single men of Silver Spoon Falls.

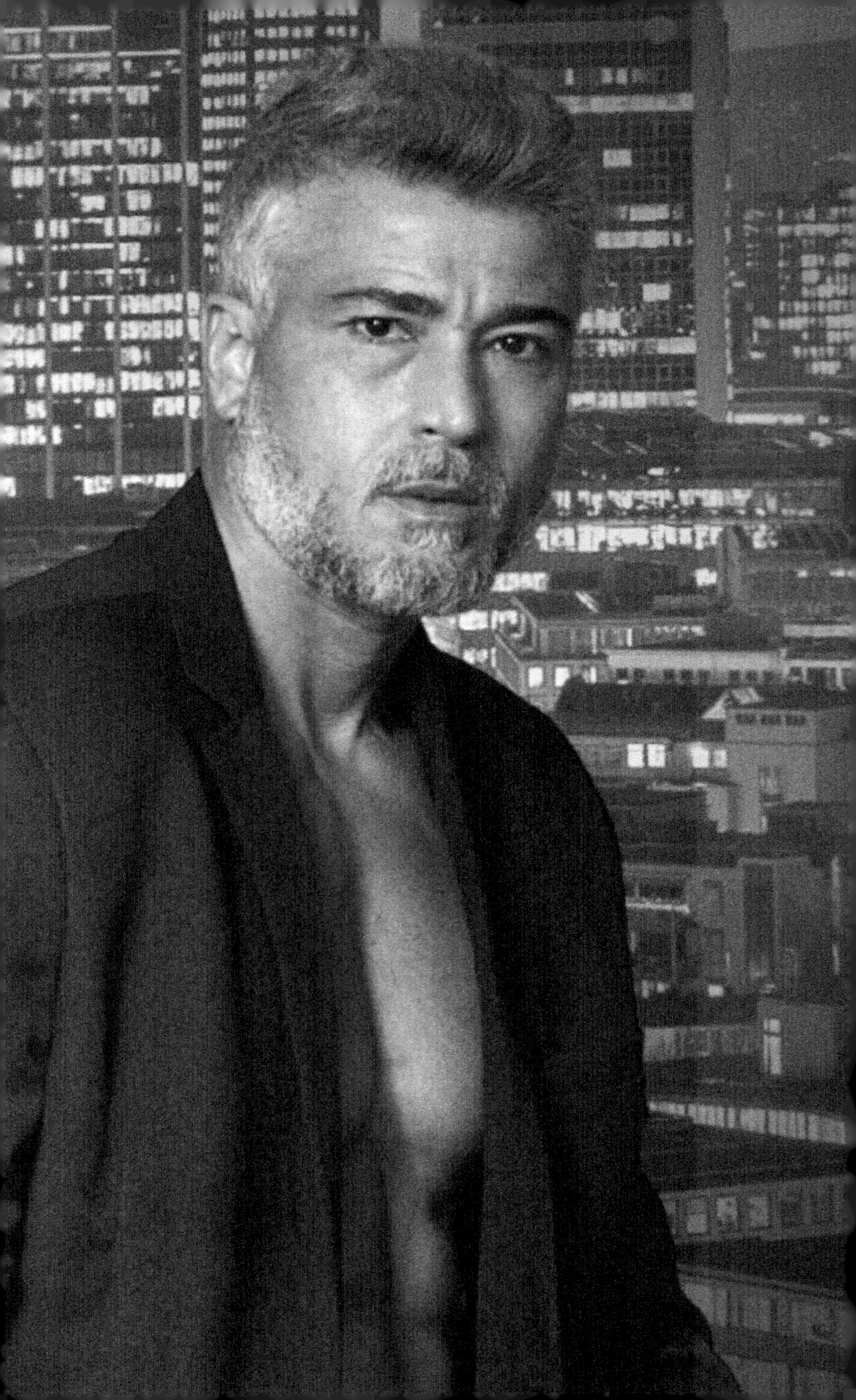

CHAPTER ONE

DANTE

"Dante?" My nephew snaps his fingers in front of my face. "Dante?" But all my attention is centered on her. The *way the fuck out of place* stunning little angel standing at the bar. Fucking hell, she's spectacular. Tiny, I'm guessing she's around five feet tall, but her generous curves make up for what she's missing in height. Her silky, dark brown hair falls in waves halfway down her back, and my fingers tingle with the need to touch the glossy strands to see if they're as soft as they look.

For some reason, I have the urge to wipe the disgusted frown off her heart-shaped face. I'm not sure what my little beauty is doing in The King's Castle, this fucking bar-slash-strip club we own with Leandro Barone, but from her expression, I'd say it isn't for entertainment.

"What the fuck is going on with you?" Dimitri, my nephew and underboss, growls, asking the same question that's going through my mind right now.

"Later," I tell him and ignore his sputtering as I stand. Somehow, I find my feet moving in her direction as if an invisible magnet is pulling me. I shove my way through the inebriated crowd with one purpose in mind. Getting to her.

Business is the last thing on my mind right this moment as I head over to meet my future. The King of the Silver Spoon Falls Underworld has just found his queen. The stunning beauty looks out of place in this bar-slash-strip club. Her snug black t-shirt shows off all her generous curves while tight blue jeans hug her curvy hips. Visions of holding on to those perfect hips while powering into her from behind flash through my mind. What the fuck? That hasn't happened to me in years. Maybe ever. Women have always been an unneeded complication for me. Between running my business empire and taking care of my niece and nephew, I don't have time for more issues.

I'm about five feet from her when some soon-to-be-dead motherfucker steps in my way and reaches for her arm. Oh, hell no. There's no way I'll ever let some other asshole touch what's mine. Even if it means I have to tear the little shit apart limb by limb and arrange to have the body hidden.

When the drunk motherfucker uses his excess body weight to trap her between his pudgy body and the bar, a red haze covers my vision. All I can think of is getting him away from my girl. I see her almond-shaped eyes widen as I step up behind the asshole and wrap my hand around the back of his neck. His dumb ass spins around and growls, "What the fuck?"

"Get the fuck out of here," I roar and watch his round face pale as he stares into my rage-filled eyes.

"Excuse me." My curvy little beauty's voice cuts through my soul. I forget about the annoying little shit and turn to her. "Who do you think you are, Gramps?" My eyes widen when her words both shock the hell out of me and turn me the fuck on. "If I want to get rid of this jerk," she points at the little asshole, "I'll tell him to get lost. I don't need some He-Man to step in." I had no idea how much sassiness turns me on. To be honest, not many people besides my niece and nephew would ever be brave enough to smart off to me. It's goddamn refreshing. "I can take care of myself," my little beauty insists.

My beautiful girl's angry yet gorgeous honey-colored eyes meet mine, and I feel my cock grow hard as I count the little freckles dotting her button nose. Fuck. I might be going off the deep end, but I don't care. This girl is totally worth losing my mind over. While my beauty and I have our stare down, I notice the asshole slinking away out of the corner of my eye. I guess his sense of self-preservation finally kicked in.

"I'm not about to let some asshole get away with manhandling you," I growl, wondering if I'm on some damn hidden camera show. This shit is fucking nuts. I never imagined finding my future in a goddamn strip club. Actually, I never really thought I'd find a woman who could wake up my heart.

"It's really none of your business," my angel argues.

"I'm making it my business." I lean close and inhale, dragging her sweet scent into my nose. Her sweet, delicate fragrance nearly brings me to my knees. I forget everything happening around us and concentrate on her.

"Dr. Girardi? What are you doing here?" Another asshole interrupts us. I glance over and see one of our regulars standing way the fuck too close to my beauty. He's the hospital administrator who loves to spend all his family's money on hookers and coke. And those are two things I keep out of my club. I don't care if patrons partake elsewhere, but I'm not about to have our barely-covered-under-the-law backroom gambling exposed by allowing working girls and dealers in here.

"Mr. Elton, I'm here to meet a friend." My little angel doesn't seem surprised to see the other man here, and she doesn't seem too scared of the fucker either. Then it hits me what he called her.

Ignoring the other man, I glance down at my curvy little beauty and raise an eyebrow. "Dr. Girardi? Are you old enough to be a doctor?"

"Aren't you too old to be getting into bar fights?" she returns without missing a beat, and my cock grows impossibly harder. I reach down and pull my jacket closed to hide the evidence of what she's doing to me.

"Oh, little beauty, I can see you're going to give me a run for my money." It's fucking true. The curvy little doctor stole my heart the first second I laid eyes on her beautiful body, and I couldn't be happier. I haven't felt this alive in years.

"Uncle Dante?" Dmitri walks up and mumbles under his breath, "Can we take this into the back room?"

I finally pull my head out of my ass, realizing we're the center of attention in this packed bar. Fuck. Meeting my little beauty has turned me into a moron. She blew my years of conditioning to hide my emotions right out of the water within seconds.

I rub the back of my neck, realizing I need to get control of my emotions. I have all the time in the world to convince my little doctor to give me a chance, but I have to do it strategically. I have everyday "business" issues as well as cartel problems on my plate already. If I'm going to make this work, I have to keep her safe. The only way to do that is to plan my wooing.

"That's a good idea," I tell Dmitri and place my hand at the base of my little beauty's spine. "Why don't you come with us." It's not really a question so I don't give her the opportunity to refuse. I feel her spine stiffen as we head through the packed strip club, leaving the little weasel standing at the bar behind us. As we enter the private back hallway, I signal for one of my enforcers to remove the trash.

Dmitri uses his fingerprint to open my office door and holds it open for us to enter. Once the door closes behind us, my little beauty turns to me. "I don't remember agreeing to come in here with you," she sputters, and I see anger flash in her honey-colored eyes. It's refreshing to find someone who doesn't seem to be frightened of me.

"I made that decision for you because I want to talk to you in private," I tell her simply, but there's nothing simple about the feelings coursing through me. Plus, my biggest priority is keeping her safe.

"I can't imagine what we could have to talk about." She slams her hands down on her curvy hips, and I barely resist the urge to smile at the defiant tilt of her chin. I glance over at Dmitri and find him standing next to the door with a smirk on his face. The fucker is enjoying the show.

"First of all, I'd like to know your name. We can start with the basics and move on from there." My voice drops as I make my intentions clear. "Then we can really get acquainted."

"I'll give you the basics." She lifts her chin and glares at me adorably. "Annabelle Girardi, twenty-eight, ER doctor, moved to Silver Spoon Falls for a job in the Emergency Department a few months ago, no family except for a distant cousin in New York." She spouts off those details before adding, "And I can't imagine there's any reason for you to have me back here. I have every right to be in this bar, and I'm not causing trouble." Oh, little beauty. *You are causing trouble.* You're changing my entire future.

"Annabelle." I hold out my hand to her and give her the same basics about myself. "I'm Dante Arakas, forty-five, businessman, and I also moved to Silver Spoon Falls recently. I have a niece and nephew in town. And you and I are going to get very well-acquainted." I see her eyes widen when I confirm my identity. It's not a shock that she recognizes my name. There probably isn't a person in the entire state who hasn't heard of me. And ninety-nine-point-nine percent fear me. It's a reputation I've cultivated over the years to maintain control of my business empire while keeping the fucking cartels at bay. Too bad, the leader of a newer cartel decided to take his chances and challenge me on my territory.

"Mr. Arakas." My little beauty doesn't appear at all concerned that she's all alone in a back room with two unfamiliar men. I can see making sure she's safe is going to be a full-time job. Dr. Annabelle Girardi is going to keep me on my toes.

"Call me Dante," I insist as our palms touch and sparks fill the air around us. When she pulls away suddenly, I let go but instantly miss the feel of her soft skin against mine.

"I don't want to call you anything except history." My little beauty's lips might lie, but her expressive eyes are telling a whole different story. "May I leave now?"

Dmitri steps closer to me and whispers, "You are so fucked. I thought Jude was blowing smoke when he warned us that the water in Silver Spoon Falls would be detrimental to our single status, but the fucker was right on in your case."

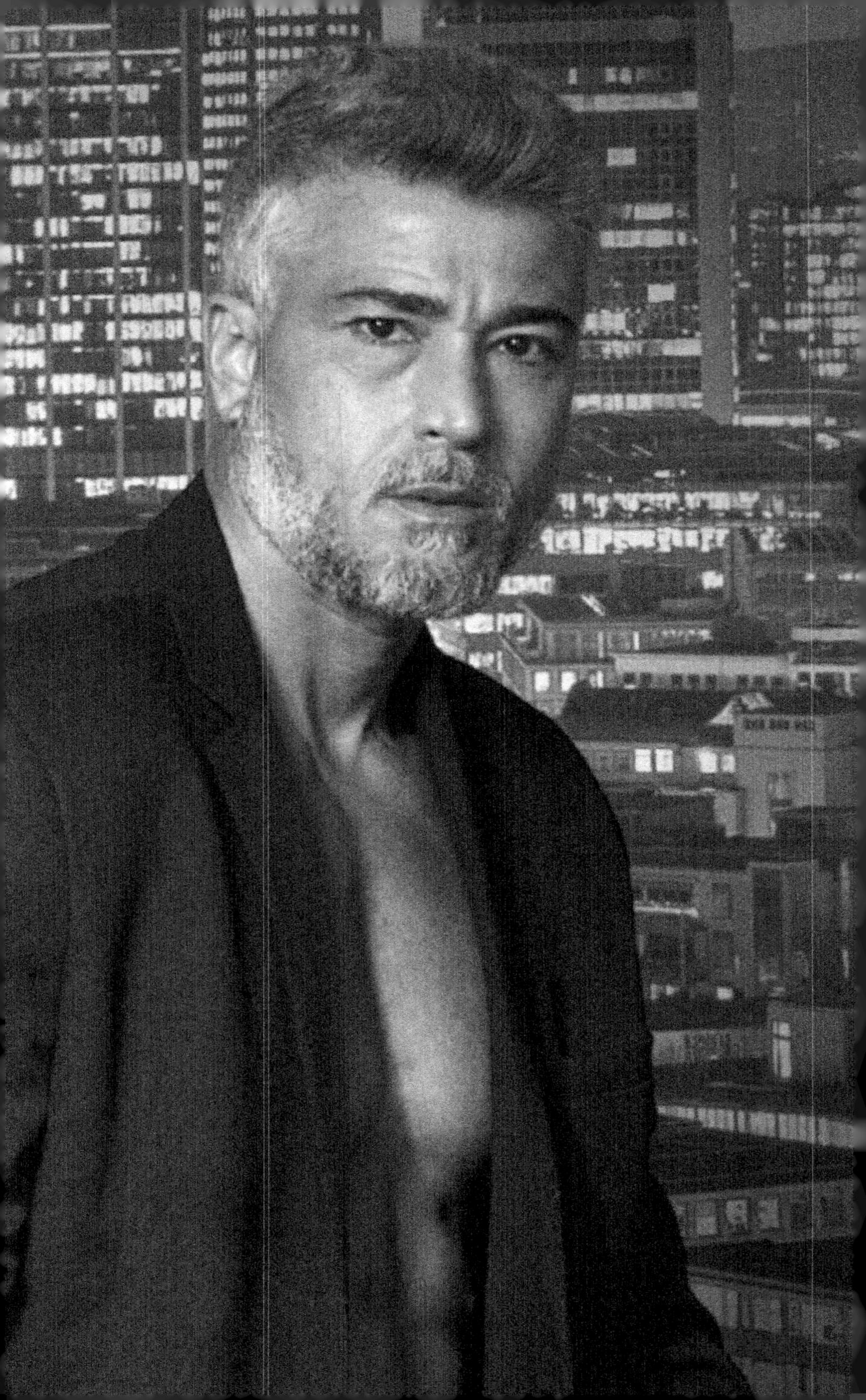

CHAPTER
TWO
BELLE

SILVER SPOON UNDER WORLD

Holy crud on a cracker. My stupid body doesn't care if the smoking hot older man is one of the biggest mobsters in the country. Even standing several feet away, I can feel my girly parts tingling from his nearness. Frustrated with him for hauling me to this back room, and with myself for my body's response to his closeness, my hand clenches at my side with the urge to punch the smug, self-assured look right off his handsome face. I need to get the heck out of here before I make a fool of myself over Dante Arakas. Or get myself in a whole lot of trouble.

After a long day working in the Silver Spoon Falls General Hospital ER, all I wanted was a big glass of wine and a long bath to relax me. Instead, I let my roommate, Macy, convince me to take part in this stupid scheme. But no good deed goes unpunished. I should have kept my rear end at home, but I was too soft-hearted to ignore my roommate's pleading. I wish I'd held my ground and refused when Macy asked me to come to the strip club and spy on her new boyfriend. Instead, I dragged my tired rear-end down here, hoping to either confirm or disprove the fear that she's being cheated on really fast.

Macy was the first person I met when I moved to the small Texas town. Moving in with her might not have been my brightest idea since she tends to have more drama than a daytime soap opera. In the last few months, she's had one catastrophe after another, and every time her world falls apart, she expects me to help. I've been promising myself I'll start looking for my own place, and this time, I swear I'm going to keep that vow.

Coming here tonight was a huge mistake. When I realized the strip club was super busy, I almost turned around and left, but I was determined to follow through on my task. Before I even had the chance to look for Tony, some drunk creep tried to assault me, and the well-connected strip club owner came to my rescue. Everyone in town knows all about Dante and Dmitri Arakas. The mafia boss and his nephew caused quite a stir on the Silver Spoon Falls grapevine when they moved to the small Texas town and bought the bar right in the middle of town. The town's wealthy residents didn't appreciate them turning the bar into a strip club, either, but no one is brave enough to complain.

Speaking of his power, I should be terrified right now, but I'm not. In my heart, I know that the only threat Dante Arakas poses to me is to my heart. For some reason, my ability to resist him flies right out the window when he stares into my eyes. Telling myself I need to get the heck out of here before I get in too deep with the mob boss, I take a step back and wait for Dante Arakas to tell me what's going on.

I perk up my ears, trying to hear what the two men are saying, but I can't quite make it out.

"Annabelle." Dante Arakas glances up and stares into my eyes, interrupting my inner turmoil. "I'd like to have a private word with you before you leave."

"Belle," I correct him. When he calls me "Annabelle," I feel like I'm back in high school, getting scolded for my tardiness. "I go by Belle," I clarify before adding, "And I don't think we have anything to talk about, so I'd like to leave." My heart squeezes in my chest at the thought of him taking me at my word and showing me the door. I'm losing my freaking mind here. With the two men standing between me and the door, there's no way I'm leaving unless they allow it. I could probably scream this room down, and no one in the bar would hear me with the loud, pounding beat going on in the main room. For the first time, I realize there's barely any bar noise in here. Like none.

Dante interrupts my musing. "Belle." The way he says it sends shivers down my spine. I need to get out of here before I get myself into trouble. The kind of trouble you can never escape. "The name suits you," he tells me without commenting on my desire to leave.

The other tall, dark, and handsome man gives me a little wave and heads for the door. Although he's much closer to my age, my heart and treacherous body don't react to him at all. After he walks out and quietly shuts the door, I feel all the air in the room disappear as Dante Arakas steps way the heck too close to me.

I take a deep breath and ask. "What did you want to talk to me about?" There. That sounds reasonable. I almost give myself a pat on the back for managing to sound normal while my heart is about to pound its way out of my chest.

"So much." His evasive answer brings me to my senses. I'm out of my league here, and I need to get away. Quickly.

"What, specifically?" I look up and feel myself drowning in his dark brown eyes. Oh, man. This forty-something man has the body of a thirty-year-old. I fight the urge to melt into a puddle of goo while staring at his smoking, burn-you-with-just-a-look hotness. His black hair has a generous sprinkling of gray throughout its thick depths, and the stylish cut screams expensive. The smug expression on his handsome face is both irritating and oddly appealing to me.

He wears his expensive dark suit with an ease that most men can't pull off. The freaking suit probably costs more than my car, and it does nothing to disguise the muscular frame beneath it.

"I'd like to get to know you." His answer confuses me even more. I feel like I'm drowning in his gaze while trying to keep my head above water. As the undertow pulls me down, I realize all my defenses are falling.

"What does that mean?" I'm way the heck out of my element here, but I'm not about to let the hot mafia boss walk all over me.

"It means I want to know everything about you." He takes my hand, and electricity blasts through my nerves, leaving me weak and disoriented. "And we can take things from there."

I open my mouth to tell him "heck no," but I can't get the words past my lips as something holds me back. "I don't think that's a good idea," I manage to squeak past the obstruction in my throat. "I'm busy with my job, and you're a…" I wonder if I'll offend him with the truth. Oh well, I don't have the ability to contain the words. "Mobster."

"I think it's the best idea I've had in a long time," he argues confidently. "We can discuss everything over dinner tomorrow night."

Talking to him is like playing ping pong. I throw my hands up in the air and growl, "I never agreed to dinner."

"But you will." He steps close and leans down to whisper in my ear, "I won't take no for an answer."

I open my mouth to tell him no, but my tongue screws up the words. "It will have to be Wednesday night. I work overnight tomorrow night." What the heck? Did I just agree to a date with the mafia boss? I might need my head examined.

"I'll make sure I'm available," He tells me and pulls out his phone. "I'll need your number and address."

A little voice in the back of my mind reminds me that I should be cautious, but I ignore it and give him my information. Then I really throw caution to the wind and let him have my phone to type in his information.

When the phone on the massive glass desk rings three times, his eyes narrow and he sighs. "I'm sorry to cut this short, but I have an issue in the bar and I don't think this club is the right environment for you." I guess that's my sign to leave.

As Dante leads me through the darkened hallway toward the back entrance, a thought occurs to me. "I need to ask you for a favor."

He looks taken aback for a second before shrugging. "Of course, I'll do anything within my power."

"I'm here tonight because my roommate thinks her boyfriend is cheating on her with one of the strippers. If I give you his information, can you check it out for me?" It might be ballsy of me to ask the mob boss for a favor the first night we meet, but oh well.

"Text me all his info and I'll see what I can do." He doesn't even blink an eye at my request. "This is Bruno, one of my bodyguards." Dante points at the massive giant who kinda resembles the Hulk. Except he's not green, or ugly. God, I need rest. "He's going to make sure you get home safely."

I open my mouth to argue but end up closing it when I realize I don't really want to stand outside alone while I wait for my Uber.

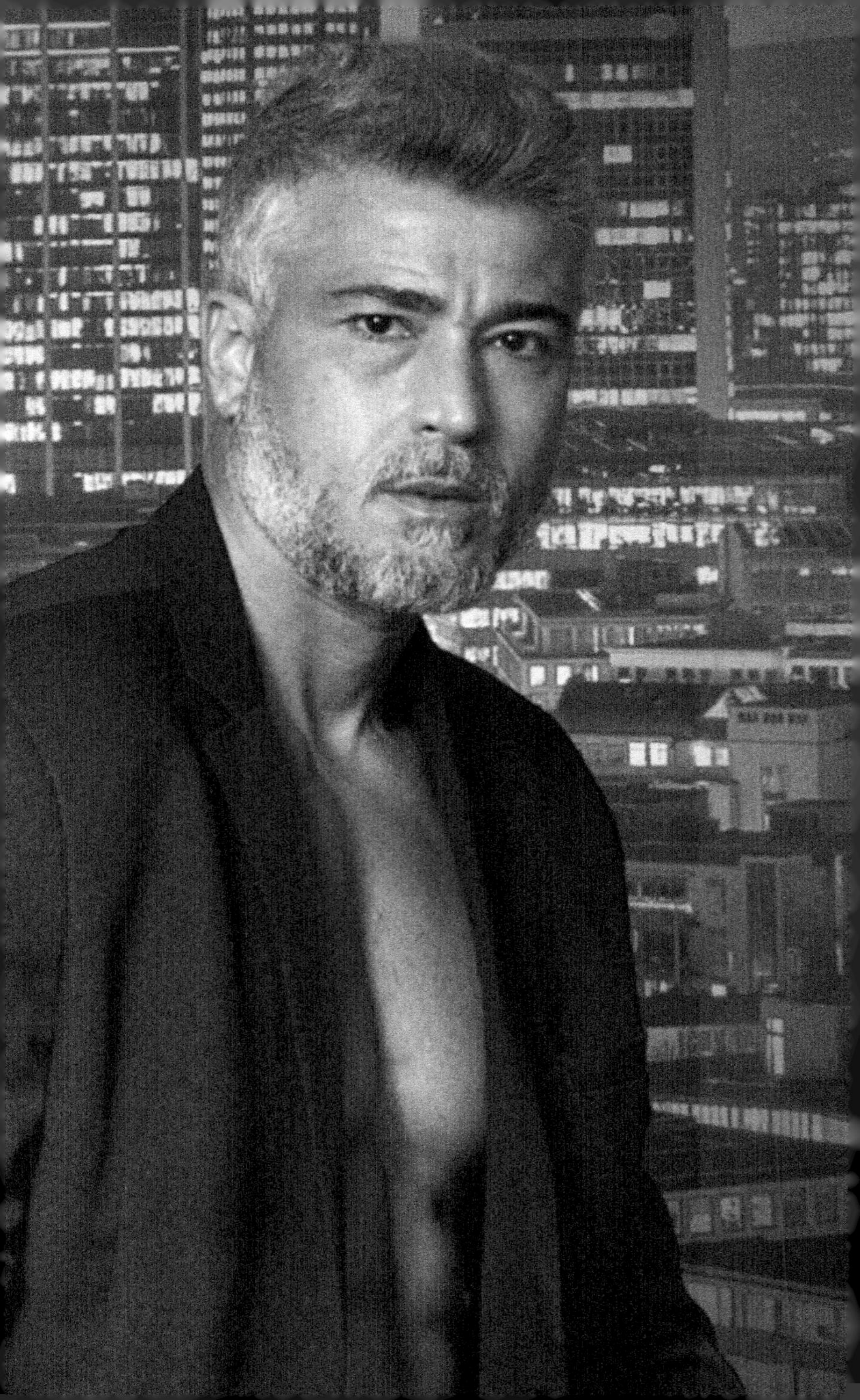

CHAPTER
THREE
DANTE

After my little beauty leaves, I hunt down Dmitri to figure out what the fuck is going on. The three rings means there are cartel-related issues.

"What happened?" I find my nephew standing at the front door with two of our bodyguards-slash-enforcers. He turns to look at me, and I see blood dotting his white shirt.

"Carmona Kings dickheads tried to sneak by the front door staff." Dmitri takes a handkerchief out of his pocket and wipes at the small red smudges on his knuckles. "I politely asked them to leave before showing them the door when they resisted."

Motherfucker. Those assholes are getting more and more brazen. It's about time I do something to cement my standing as the only underworld leader in this area.

"We're going to need to have a meeting," I tell Dmitri. "And make the appropriate plans to discourage their attempts." No telling who the fuck is listening in, so I choose my words carefully.

"I'll arrange it," Dmitri agrees and turns to head back to the offices when I stop him.

"And I need you to do me a favor." I pull out the information Belle gave me a few minutes ago. I'm relieved to hear that my girl was in this bar helping a friend out, but I don't want her to have a reason to come back. Unless she's with me in my protected office that is.

"I can't believe you're turning me into a glorified errand boy to keep a woman you just met tonight happy," Dmitri grumbles as he signals two of our men over.

"That woman is my soulmate," I tell him, ending the argument. "And I expect you to treat her as such."

"Motherfucking Silver Spoon Falls water," my nephew grumbles as he walks away. He's acting put out, but I know my nephew well. Ever since his sister found her soulmate here in Silver Spoon Falls, he's been waiting for the same thing to happen to both of us. A part of me suspects he is even looking forward to having a woman in his life.

Karma or fate or the Silver Spoon Falls water does have a horrible sense of timing, though. It dropped my soulmate into my life right in the middle of my battle to keep the Carmona Kings from weaseling in on my territory.

Five minutes later, I get a text from Bruno that my girl made it home safely. Now that I've found her, I refuse to take any chances with her safety, so Bruno is going to camp out across the street from her apartment to keep an eye on her until I can arrange for a permanent bodyguard for my little beauty.

I spend the next day planning to woo and protect Belle. Every time my phone vibrates, a thrill shoots through me at the thought that my little beauty is texting me. Unfortunately, none of the messages are from her, which kills my good mood.

When Dmitri gives me undisputable evidence that her roommate's sleazeball boyfriend has been fucking one of our strippers, I finally have the excuse to text my girl. Fuck. She's turning me into a goddamn teenager.

I pull out my phone and send a picture to Belle.

> your roommate needs to kick this dick to the curb.

I count the seconds until her reply comes like a lovesick puppy.

BELLE

> I need to kick my roommate to the curb, too.

My little beauty doesn't have to worry about getting rid of her roommate. That will be taken care of when I move Belle into my place. The quick report Dmitri pulled on Belle gave me just enough information to know that my girl isn't going to be happy with me interfering with her life. My independent little beauty put herself through college and medical school on scholarships and by working two jobs after her parents died in a car accident.

Belle won't have to fight to take care of herself any longer. That's my job now. I'm sure she's going to give me a fight when I step in, but she'll get over it. Her safety and happiness are now my biggest concern.

She has an unbelievable hold on my heart. My little beauty occupies my mind every second of the day, and I have a hard time concentrating on business. Dmitri seems amused by my predicament while the rest of my men are dumbfounded.

After the last meeting of the day finally comes to an end, I sit back and take a deep breath while I think about my little beauty.

"You need to go kidnap your girl and lock her up somewhere so you can get your head back in the game." Dmitri hands me a glass of my favorite whiskey. "We have to figure out this cartel shit before the fuckers get any more brazen."

I know he's right. "It kills me to admit that you're right," I admit. "But you're right. Nothing else seems important except her." My nephew's eyebrows shoot up at my declaration, and I force myself to ask, "You think I'm nuts, don't you?"

"Not at all." Dmitri shakes his head. "I've been watching all the assholes in town drop like flies for months. It doesn't really shock me that the love bug struck you, too."

"Don't worry, the water in this goddamn town will get you soon enough," I warn him. It's the town's claim to fame. An insane number of the residents in town are happily shackled to their soulmates who they fell in love with at first sight. Up until I laid eyes on Belle, I thought it was a crazy urban legend. Well, that fairytale just bit me in the ass. "Then you'll understand what I'm going through," I threaten him with reality.

"Oh, fuck no." My nephew's eyes widen as he shakes his head vigorously. "I'm only drinking bottled water from now on," he growls and adds under his breath but still loud enough for me to hear, "I don't want to turn into a moron like you and all the other pussy-whipped assholes in town."

Not long ago, Dmitri's sister, Devin, decided to hide out in Silver Spoon Falls. I almost had a heart attack when my niece disappeared, but my contacts found her in the small Texas town almost immediately. The Carmona Kings were increasing their attacks on us, so I decided to leave Devin here and keep a close eye on her. To my surprise, she caught the eye of a powerful, well-connected lawyer, Jude Despora, and the rest was history.

Sitting back and watching their relationship develop without interfering was one of the hardest things I've ever done, but it was necessary. My niece has a good head on her shoulders, and I was forced to let her use it. In the end, we added a powerful MC to our list of allies and a powerful lawyer who loves my niece infinitely to the family.

Once I add my curvy little doctor to the family and get rid of the cartel threat, I will be able to breathe easy and maybe retire to make babies with my little beauty.

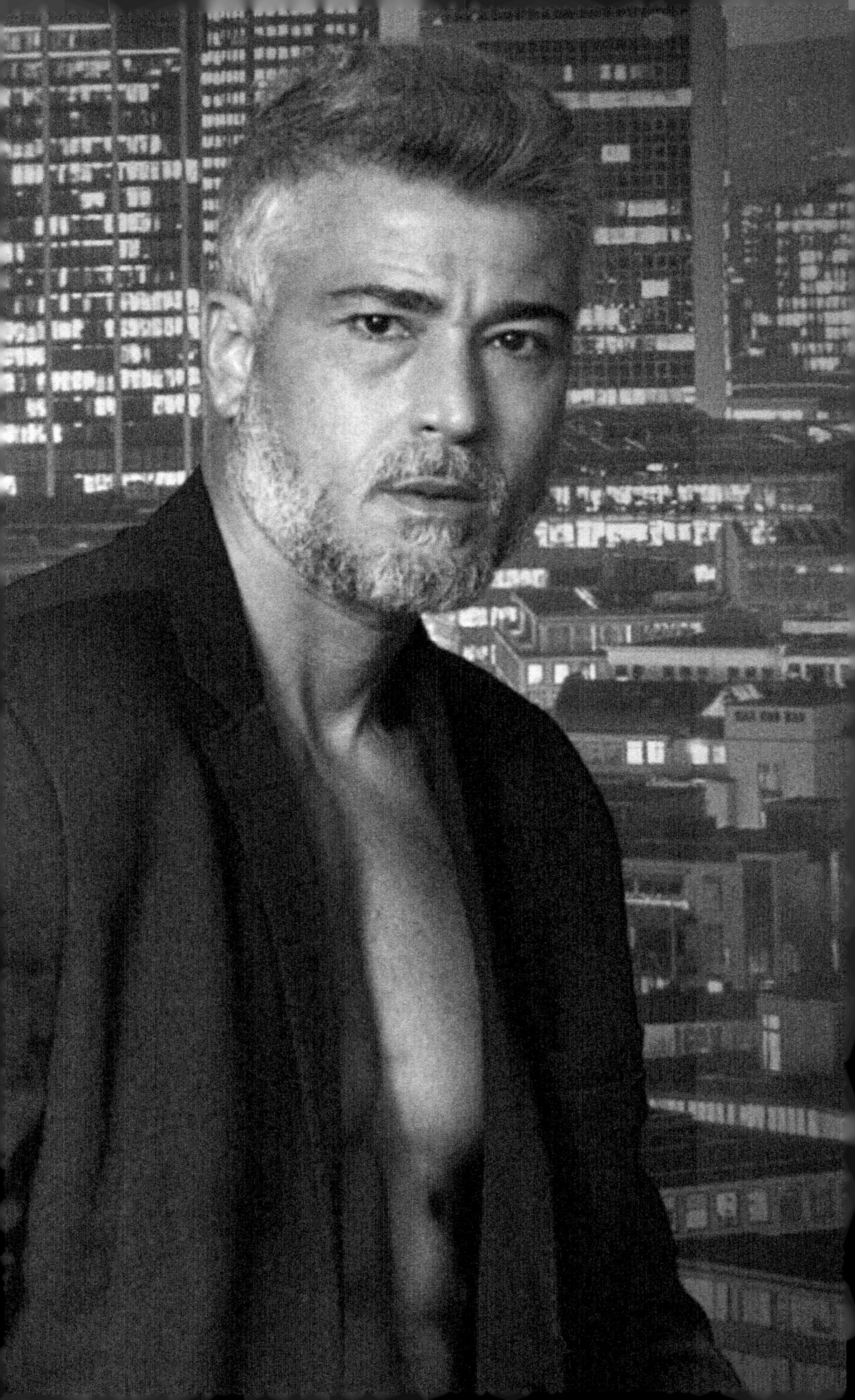

CHAPTER FOUR

DANTE

At six o'clock, I give up trying to get anything else done. My chest aches while my limbs feel unusually heavy. A foggy sensation wraps around me as I admit to myself that I fucking feel like shit on a cracker. Rubbing the back of my neck, I pull out my phone to shoot Dmitri a quick text.

> I'm going to head out for a while.

DMITRI

> Couldn't take it anymore?

> Something like that.

DMITRI

> I'll be here. Working. You might try it sometime.

Asshole. If I was feeling better, I'd kick his ass for that remark. I barely make it to the car when things turn to shit big fucking time.

Ever since our afternoon meeting, I've had pain radiating through my chest and up the back of my neck. I wasn't too worried about it, figuring the pain is stress combined with missing my little beauty. But the black dots swimming in front of my eyes and overwhelming nausea have me thinking something else is going on.

"Take me to the hospital," I order Bruno seconds before everything around me goes black.

I wake up to find bright lights shining in my eyes and a pimply-faced fucker smiling down at me.

"Mr. Arakas, I'm Dr. Altman. Don't worry, we're going to take care of you." What the fuck? He's even younger than my angel. Either I'm way the fuck too old or doctors seem to be getting younger.

A male tech rushes into the room pushing a white machine. "We're going to do a quick EKG to check your heart." This fucker cuts my shirt off like it's nothing and shakes his head sadly as he stares at my chest. "There's no way the stickers will work on your chest. I don't want to take the time to shave you, so we'll just make it work."

"Wait." This has gone too far. I'm feeling much fucking better. At least, I thought I was until I attempt to sit up and the room starts to spin. Fucking hell. I drop back onto the hard-as-hell bed and take several deep breaths, trying to keep my lunch down. I'm not sure what hurts worse, the nervous nurse poking the hell out of me with needles or this asshole and his stickers from hell. I wish for the darkness to overtake me again as the pain multiplies from every direction. Is every motherfucker who works at this hospital in my room right now? When the efficient EKG tech places a white sticker on my chest and rips it off, taking all the hair around it too, I've had enough.

"Fucking stop," I growl, but my voice is so fucking weak, I'm not sure anyone hears me. The asshole tearing the skin off my chest doesn't even pause. He continues doing the same thing to several spots across my chest. My chest pain has quadrupled by the time he gets all the little stickers attached. Bruno stands in the corner typing away on his phone while the fucking assholes torture me.

The tech takes a pair of scissors and slices through my favorite pair of pants, but I'm too fucking weak to stop him. He uses the fucking torture stickers to rip clumps of hair off each of my calves, and I wonder how much more pain I'm going to endure. I can't believe I'm going to goddamn die right after finding my soulmate. Karma really is a fucking bitch.

"Don't worry. We'll save your life, and the hair will grow back," the technician rattles on while attaching wires to all the little stickers. "Now, lie back and stay still while the test runs," he tells me. Like I have any choice in the matter.

Once the machine spits out a long sheet of paper, the asshole hands the paper to the little shit doctor. "Don't worry, you're in good hands," he tells me and pushes the machine out the door as I rub my sore goddamn chest. What the hell?

"Fucking hell." I sit back, wondering if I'm about to meet my end here in the Silver Spoon Falls General Hospital.

"What happened." Belle storms into the room, and I instantly feel peace as my eyes roam over her luscious curves that are half-hidden behind the loose white lab coat. Even a goddamn heart attack can't keep my cock down when she's in the room. The fucker turns hard as a rock, and I shift to make sure the goddamn thin sheet they threw over me covers the evidence of my arousal.

"I don't know," I tell her honestly while my fucking sluggish mind tries to get with the program.

"What do you mean?" Worry flashes through Belle's honey eyes as she walks over to glare at me. "Tell me what you know."

"I was fine one minute, and the next, I was in here getting tortured." My attempt to explain is weak at best.

"Don't worry. I'm going to take care of you," Belle promises me and runs her hand through my hair. I might be at death's door, but her touch still sends electricity flowing through my veins while my soul fills with peace. I'm sounding like a goddamn greeting card.

"This is a hell of a way to get to see you," I joke, trying to lighten the situation, but my attempt falls flat and Belle frowns down at me.

Dmitri forces his way into my room followed by Devin and her husband, a member of the Silver Spoon MC, and his MC brother, Hands Grimes, a pediatric surgeon. "I want to know what the fuck is going on," my nephew demands as my girl steps over to talk to Dr. Grimes.

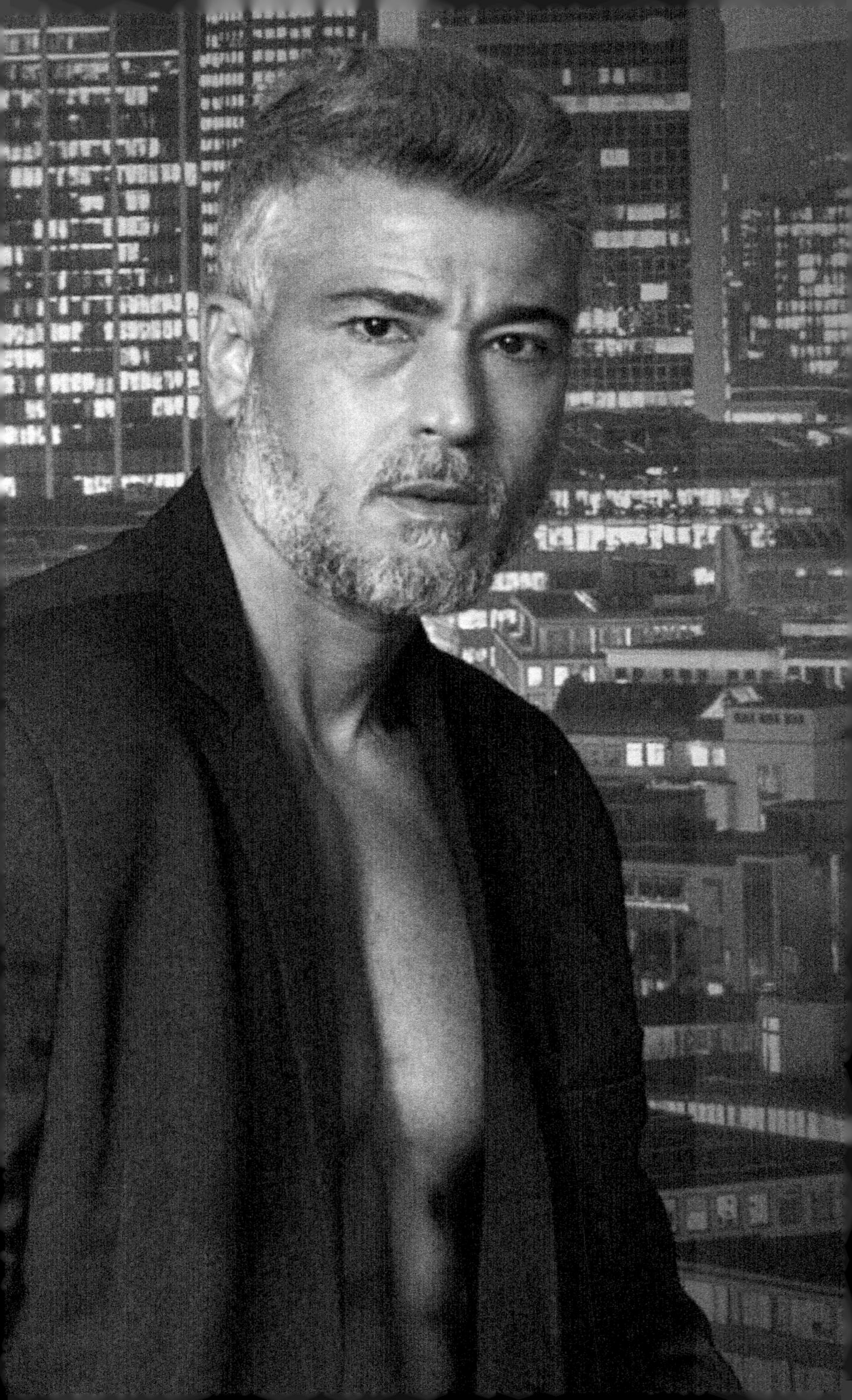

CHAPTER
FIVE
BELLE

My heart nearly stopped when I saw his name on the hospital chart. Seeing the powerful mob boss weak and disoriented almost brought me to my knees. Oh, man. I instantly know two things. I'm in over my head here, and there's a good chance I'm going to get my heart crushed by him. It's already too late for me to put a halt to this situation. Dante Arakas stole my heart the first moment we met.

I was so worried when I rushed into the room, I barely noticed his naked, muscular chest or the large bulge hidden beneath the thin sheet. Now that I've had time to calm down, I'm about to self-combust from the sight of Dante Arakas half-naked on the hospital gurney.

When his lab work comes back, I get a surprise. The forty-five-year-old mob boss isn't having a heart attack. He's been poisoned. I see a lot of sprains, broken bones, and even motor vehicle accident victims, but I haven't had a poisoning victim since medical school. I end up consulting with two experts in the field to make sure I give Dante the best shot at a full recovery.

Dmitri Arakas slams his fist into the wall when I give them the news. "Motherfucking hell. Those cartel assholes must've gotten into The King's Castle."

Things go into overdrive after that. Men in black suits and law enforcement fill the small emergency department, and we end up diverting all medical emergencies to the nearest town.

We start aggressive treatments to make sure Dante doesn't suffer any long-term effects while the authorities begin their investigation. It's the longest night of my freaking life as I end up spending most of it in the ICU with my handsome mob boss.

Three days later, I'm ready to suffocate the big jerk with a pillow. He's the freaking worst patient I've ever had. "Are you trying to be this annoying or does it come naturally?" I growl as he glares at me. Freaking hell.

"I'm going to show you what comes naturally when we get home," Dante promises me, and I almost melt at the heated look he throws my way. Out of the corner of my eye, I notice Dmitri smirking and nearly choke on the overabundance of testosterone swirling around the large hospital room.

Once Dante was out of the woods, we transferred him to one of the hospital's private suites. "Who said I'm going home with you?" I argue, knowing it's a useless gesture. I'm slowly getting used to his tendency to get his way.

"Until we get this situation under control, I'm not letting you out of my sight." Dante is back to his pre-poisoned, bossy self. In fact, looking at him now, no one would ever be able to tell he was on death's door a few days ago.

"I don't remember agreeing to this." I've found that giving him hell is my favorite pastime.

"You expressed your agreement when you spent every night since my poisoning curled up in the hospital bed next to me." Dante has a point, but I still refuse to let him win too easily. It sets a bad precedent if I let him have his way right out the gate.

"Everything is in place for your discharge," Dmitri walks up and informs Dante. After this went down, I got to see the full power of the Arakas Family. In my mind, I knew they were one of the most powerful families in the country, but I didn't equate what I knew of them with the man who I'd met and fallen for. Evidently, they'd been in the process of building a protected fortress on the outskirts of town. In the meantime, Dante and Dmitri have been staying in a penthouse close to the strip club. When the cartel got someone close enough to poison Dante, they took the threat seriously and pooled their resources. Somehow, they were able to convince the builder to work day and night to finish one of the main buildings on the compound.

"Did you bring everything you'll need for a while?" Dante turns to me and raises an eyebrow. Darn. I realize I'm about to have a huge fight with the mob boss.

"No." Dead silence meets my answer. "I never agreed to move in with you." His tendency to assume he's going to get his way is really freaking annoying.

"You don't have a choice." Dante slams his hand down on the bedside table. "I'll kidnap you if I have to."

Dmitri looks back and forth between us before smirking. "I'm going to step out and get a coffee while you two work this out." Dmitri has been around throughout Dante's entire hospital stay, but he somehow manages to stay on the sidelines. It's scary how fast I'm becoming accustomed to their crazy lifestyle.

I hold my own fighting Dante's demands until he pulls out the big guns. "I know this is happening quickly, and I'd like to give you more time to get used to this situation, but I don't have the fucking time." Not exactly the most romantic declaration, but his actions over the last few days have shown me that the mob boss really is serious about me. Scarily serious.

My heart might never be the same again if things don't work out between us, but I know I'm going to give him a chance. He's saying all the right things, and hopefully, he really means them. "My enemies could use you to get to me." Dante runs his hands through my hair and pulls my face close to his, bringing my attention back to him. "You can have your own room, and I'll try to give you space." My heart melts, watching the powerful mob boss negotiate. "But I have to know you're safe. Plus, you're getting away from your pain in the ass roommate."

I guess that is one huge positive to this situation. Then he kisses me to within an inch of my life. As his tongue explores my mouth, I actually forget all about what we're talking about and kiss him back with all the pent-up desire and worry I've been feeling the last few days.

Before I let him have his way, I make sure he knows where I stand. "I'm not quitting my job." I've worked too freaking hard to give up my career now. "But I'll stay at your compound." Although I'm giving in awfully easy, I can't seem to stop myself.

"We'll discuss your job later." Oh yes, we will, Mr. Mob Boss. He might think he's winning, but Dante has a surprise coming.

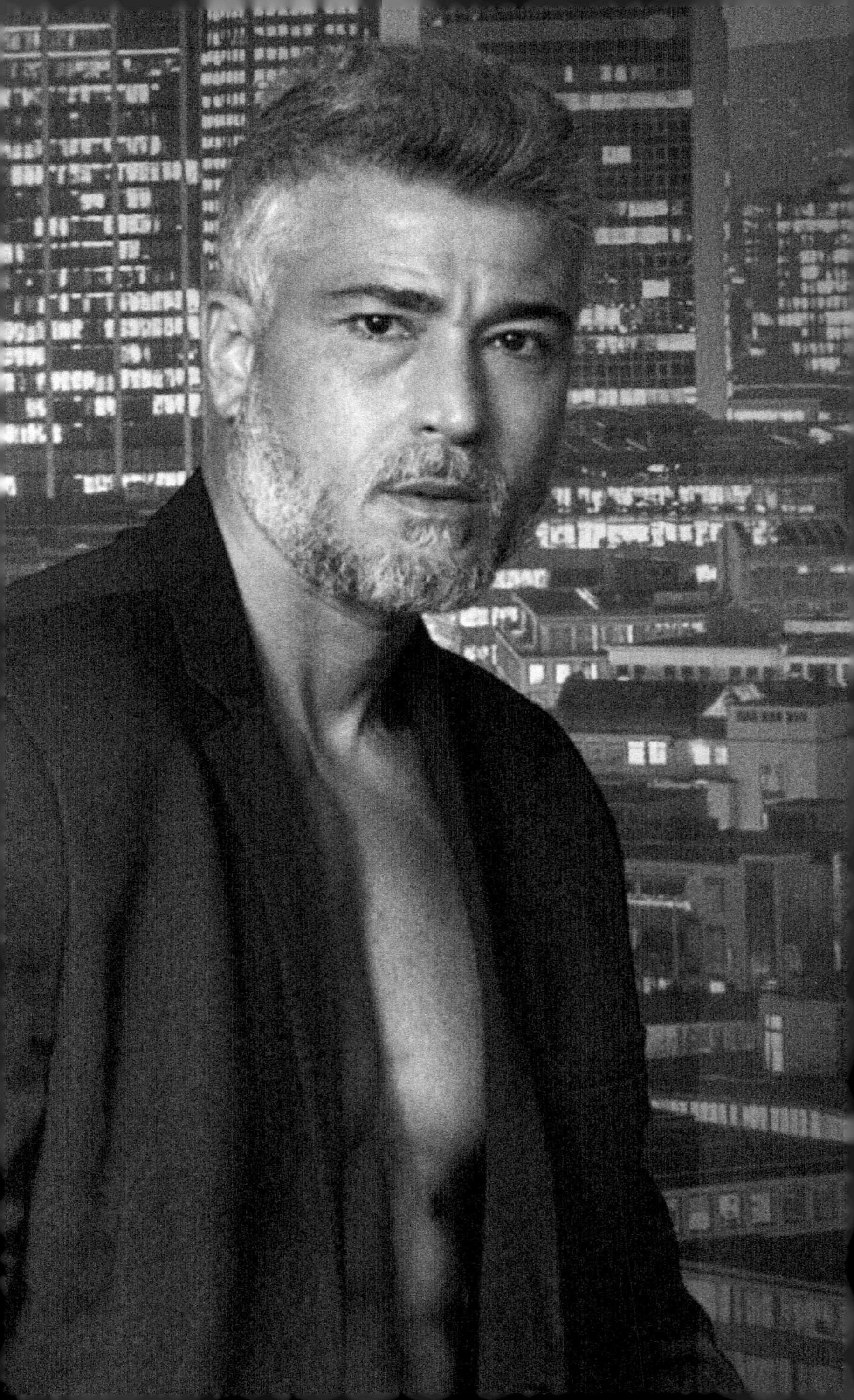

CHAPTER
SIX
BELLE

Over the next two weeks, most of my stuff makes its way to Dante's new home. I'm not really sure how it happened, but I'm powerless to stop it. Since I'm not going to have to pay rent for the foreseeable future, I use some of my savings to pay my half of the rent for the remainder of my lease with Macy, telling myself I'll find another place if things don't work out with Dante. Macy gives me a hard time for abandoning her, but I have too much on my plate to worry about how she's going to deal.

I move my things into the bedroom across the hall from Dante's room, but I'm hoping to actually move into his big suite soon. I continue working my shifts at the hospital, and Dante insists on sending a freaking entourage with me every time. Two bodyguards ride with me, and two follow behind us. When we arrive at the hospital, the bodyguards go through this crazy routine of checking out the entire emergency department before I'm allowed to go in. Once they're sure the hospital is safe, they melt into the background while I work. It's all surreal, but I've gotten used to the looks I get whenever I go anywhere with my troupe.

The Silver Spoon Falls grapevine has been steadily buzzing with news of our relationship, and I'm pretty sure there isn't a flea on a horse's rear end who doesn't know that I've moved in with the mob boss.

We spend all my free evenings together, and to my shock, he's respected my boundaries. Almost too well. Every night, he kisses me to within an inch of my life, and then he tucks me into my room without making a move on me. If I'm honest with myself, I admit that I'm starting to get a little tired of the chaste nature of our relationship.

I'm sitting in his massive library reading a medical journal when the door slams open. "What in the fuck were you thinking, wearing a little piece of nothing in front of my men?" I almost laugh at the absurd accusation, but Dante's red, angry face tells me he isn't going to take that response well.

"What?" My usually agile brain shuts down at the sight of my handsome mob boss spitting fire. At me. I should be terrified, but it turns me the heck on to see his chest rising and falling rapidly while his dark brown eyes practically glow with rage.

"I saw the video of you swimming in the goddamn outdoor pool wearing next to nothing." Dante has lost his ever-loving mind.

"Next to nothing?" I poke my finger into his chest as my anger steadily grows. Mr. Mob Boss isn't the only one in this relationship with a temper. "I wouldn't have been more covered in a nun's habit." I can't believe he's upset about me wearing a very conservative one-piece bathing suit to swim in the pool he had installed for me. Either he's losing his mind or I am.

"I don't want my men to see you in any less than a fucking habit." Dante sighs and runs his hand through his thick hair. "You've turned me into a lunatic," he admits and wraps his arms around me. "Please, have patience with me while I adjust to these new circumstances."

"New circumstances?" My anger steadily dissipates as he hugs me close and runs his nose along my neck.

"Having a beauty to protect," Dante admits and covers my lips with his. I melt into his embrace as desire replaces my anger. His hands run over my back, sending little sparks shooting down my spine. Oh no, my handsome mob boss isn't going to get me all hot and bothered and then walk away. Not this time.

Dante tries to lift his head, but I grab the back of his head and growl, "If you stop now, I'm going to kill you." I freaking mean it. Frustration is a bitch.

Shock flashes through his dark brown eyes, turning them fiery. For once, I actually get to witness my confident mob boss at a loss for words.

His mouth opens and closes a few times before he finally mutters, "Are you sure?"

"Positive." I run my tongue along his stubbly chin and press my body against his hardness. "Now get a move on, gramps."

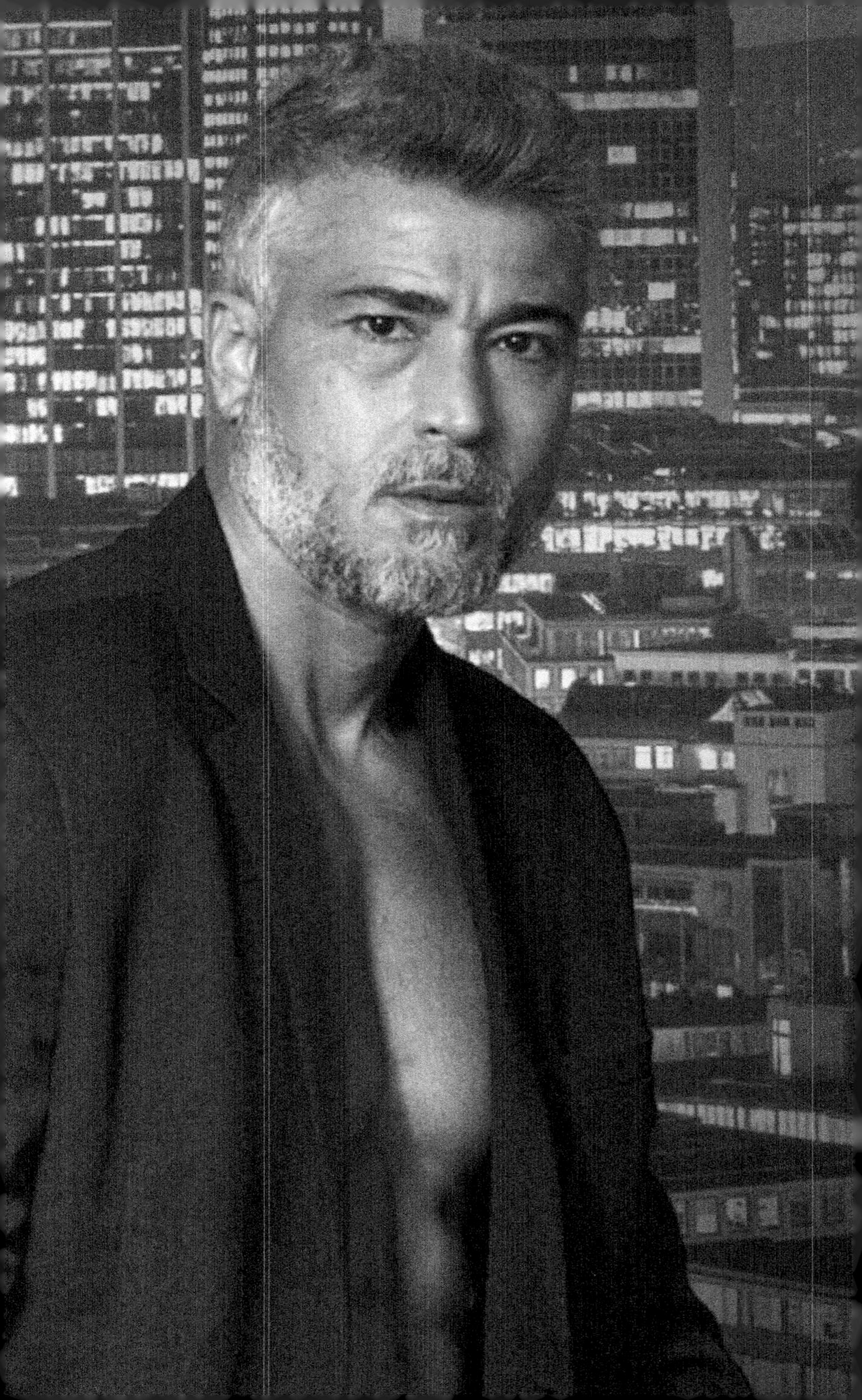

CHAPTER
SEVEN
DANTE

F uck me. My cock nearly tears a hole through the front of my pants when my beauty's words echo around the room. I smile against her lips before smacking one of her luscious ass cheeks. "You're going to pay for that." God, all my dreams are about to come true. Giving her time to get used to our new relationship before making a move has been killing me.

"Promises, promises." Belle smiles as she reaches between us to wrap her soft hand around my cock, catching my attention big fucking time. My curvy little love sure isn't shy. She's fucking perfect for me. Even through the expensive material, her warm touch almost brings me to my knees.

"Hold on, little beauty." I kiss her soft lips while my hands roam over her luscious curves. I've wanted her for so long, I don't even know where to start.

"You hold on, gramps." My sassy girl winks before dropping to her knees in front of me. Fuck me. Belle is trying to run the show. I knew it was unlikely that my twenty-eight-year-old soulmate was untouched, but having proof of her experience nearly brings me to my knees.

"I didn't expect you to be this forward. Or experienced," I manage to growl as the thought of another man educating my beauty sends murderous rage coursing through me.

"I actually don't have any real experience," Belle assures me but acts anything but inexperienced when she reaches into my pants and frees my rock-hard erection. "It's all book knowledge." She glances up and winks. "My college roommate thought it was her duty to make sure I had the proper education on giving a blow job." The feel of her soft hand wrapping around my erection is almost too much for me to take. "We watched videos, and I'm very good at taking notes." Right this second, I'm very appreciative of her college roommate's foresight.

As her sweet lips wrap around my cock, I lock my knees and grab the back of her head. Belle sucks timidly at first, then a little harder as her confidence grows. Part of me never wants this to end, but I'm not sure how long I'll be able to let her experiment. My fucking control is slipping fast. When she wraps her soft hand around my balls and gently massages them, I know I'm nearing the point of no control.

I use my grip on her head to give her a gentle tug. "Have mercy. I'm an old man." I wink and lift her up against my body. As her silky legs wrap around my waist, I close my eyes and take several deep breaths, trying to bring my raging hunger under control.

"I wasn't done," Belle complains against my lips.

"I'll let you finish another time," I promise. "You won't have to twist my arm."

"What if I want to twist something else?" Belle rubs her luscious curves against me, sending all the blood in my body straight to my cock.

I kiss her soft lips before laying her across the bed. "You can twist away next time, but I'm in charge this time."

"I can live with that." My little beauty sighs as I place a kiss on her nose before stepping back to rip away my clothes.

Her gorgeous eyes widen almost comically when I drag my dress pants and boxers down my hips, giving her a good look at my hard-as-nails cock. "Oh, man." She bites her bottom lip while staring at my erection.

"Please tell me you aren't having second thoughts," I groan, praying I'm not about to need an ice-cold shower to bring myself under control.

"Nope." My brave little beauty smiles up at me. "I'm just enjoying the scenery." She never fails to surprise me.

"I'm glad to hear that." I stalk over to the bed and start slowly removing her clothes. As each inch of her luscious body comes into view, I feel my cock grow impossibly harder. I'm embarrassed to say my hands shake when I reach for the hook on the front of her pink lacy bra.

"You're fucking gorgeous," I tell my beauty.

"You're not so bad yourself, gramps." She insists on pressing my buttons, and I fucking love every second of it. "I just hope you can keep up with me." Belle smirks, and I barely resist the urge to spank her sweet ass.

"You're begging for a spanking," I threaten before leaning down to kiss the soft skin above her belly button. Love and possessiveness combine within my soul as I stare down at my luscious soulmate.

"You keep making all these threats... I mean, promises, but you haven't really followed through on any of them." When she looks into my eyes and winks, I have no doubt in my mind that she's going to keep me on my toes for the next fifty years or so.

It's time for me to show my little beauty who's in charge. "Hold on while I make good on my threats." I spread her silky thighs and lean down to run my tongue along the skin above her shaved pussy.

My little beauty arches her back and cries out when I run my finger through the wetness dripping from her cunt while sucking on her clit. She calls my name as I press my finger as deep as her tight walls will allow.

"Please, don't stop," she begs as her fingers twist in the bedsheets.

"Never," I promise and throw myself into blowing my little beauty's mind. My cock steadily drips cum as I lose myself in her taste. I gently press a second finger into her tight opening while sucking hard on her clit. When she comes, her silky walls flutter around my fingers. I slow my movements and let her ride out the orgasm before I start to build her up again. Her scream bounces off the walls when she comes again.

"I can't," Belle insists when I continue my movements. "Not again."

"You can and you will." I'm going to make sure my little beauty is so fucking addicted to my lovemaking that she can't even think about leaving me.

After her fourth orgasm, I give her rear end a hard smack before kissing my way up her luscious body. I stop every few inches to explore and leave a mark. After tonight, her sweet body will show evidence of my ownership.

"You're never getting away from me," I breathe against her berry-red nipple and watch as it hardens even more.

"I already knew that." Belle digs her nails into the back of my scalp and tugs. "Now, stop torturing me and show me what you can do with your impressive equipment."

I can't have my girl doubting my lovemaking ability. After kissing my way up her chest and neck, I pull her bottom lip between my teeth and bite down gently.

Belle gasps as my tongue soothes the little sting. She arches her back and cries out my name when I reach between us to pinch her tight nipple. I give the other side the same attention while my cock begs me to hurry the fuck up. Her body is my playground, and I will never get enough of it.

My tongue tangles with hers while her nails dig into my shoulders. When she wraps her hand around my hard cock and gives it a squeeze, I almost come. Damn. I wanted to take my time with her, but I'm losing control quickly. I shift my hips, pulling my fucking cock out of her grasp before lining it up with her tight opening.

"You own me." I press forward and stare down into her passion-filled eyes as I make her mine for eternity and beyond. Her silky walls tighten around my cock, and I pause, giving her time to adjust to my penetration. My brave little beauty quickly catches on and begins to move her hips up to meet my downward thrusts.

I press down hard on her clit and feel her inner muscles spasm around my cock as she comes. I slow my thrusts and let her ride out the orgasm. I'm not sure where I find the control, but I manage to hold off coming until she climaxes two more times.

I'm barely able to hold myself up when the last drop of cum blasts from my cock, but I manage to spin us around and pull Belle against my side.

The next morning, my eyes pop open as pleasure zings through my body. Belle sucks hard on my cock while softly massaging my balls. "Fuck. I can't believe I slept through part of this," I groan, fighting not to come quickly as my legs tremble from the effort.

My little beauty looks up into my eyes while slowly releasing my cock from her mouth. "You did promise me another shot to finish what I started,"

Belle reminds me and leans over to run her tongue down the front of my hard cock.

"Finish away," I manage to croak as all the blood in my body rushes to my erection.

"I plan for both of us to finish," she whispers, closing her lips back around my cock. When she swallows and allows my shaft to slide deeper down her throat, I give up the fight to hold on and come. Fucking hard. Black dots dance in front of my eyes, and I start to worry that my little beauty really did give me a heart attack.

As my breathing slows, I grab Belle under her arms and roll us both over. She squeaks when I suck hard on one of her nipples before kissing my way down her sweet body.

"Now, I'm going to enjoy my breakfast." I glance up and wink at her before spreading her pussy lips and running my tongue up her wet center. I'll never get enough of my little beauty, so I set out to blow her mind.

After I give her three more orgasms, we both pass the fuck out, and I end up sleeping until after noon. I leave her sleeping peacefully while I drag my ass down to the office to get to work.

I've been spending nearly every moment since the poisoning making sure my girl is safe. It didn't take long for us to figure out that one of the bartenders at the strip club was the Carmona Kings mole. I had impressive plans to make him suffer, but the dumb motherfucker didn't live long enough to regret his choices. The cartel silenced the bastard before we were able to find him. We learned those assholes have no sense of loyalty whatsoever. They strongly believe everyone is expendable once their usefulness is over. Fucking up the attempt on my life was the last straw for the asshole who'd managed to weasel his way into my club. We did a clean sweep of the club and removed anyone who doesn't have a proven record with our organization.

The situation is under control for now, but I'm still on edge and worried about my family.

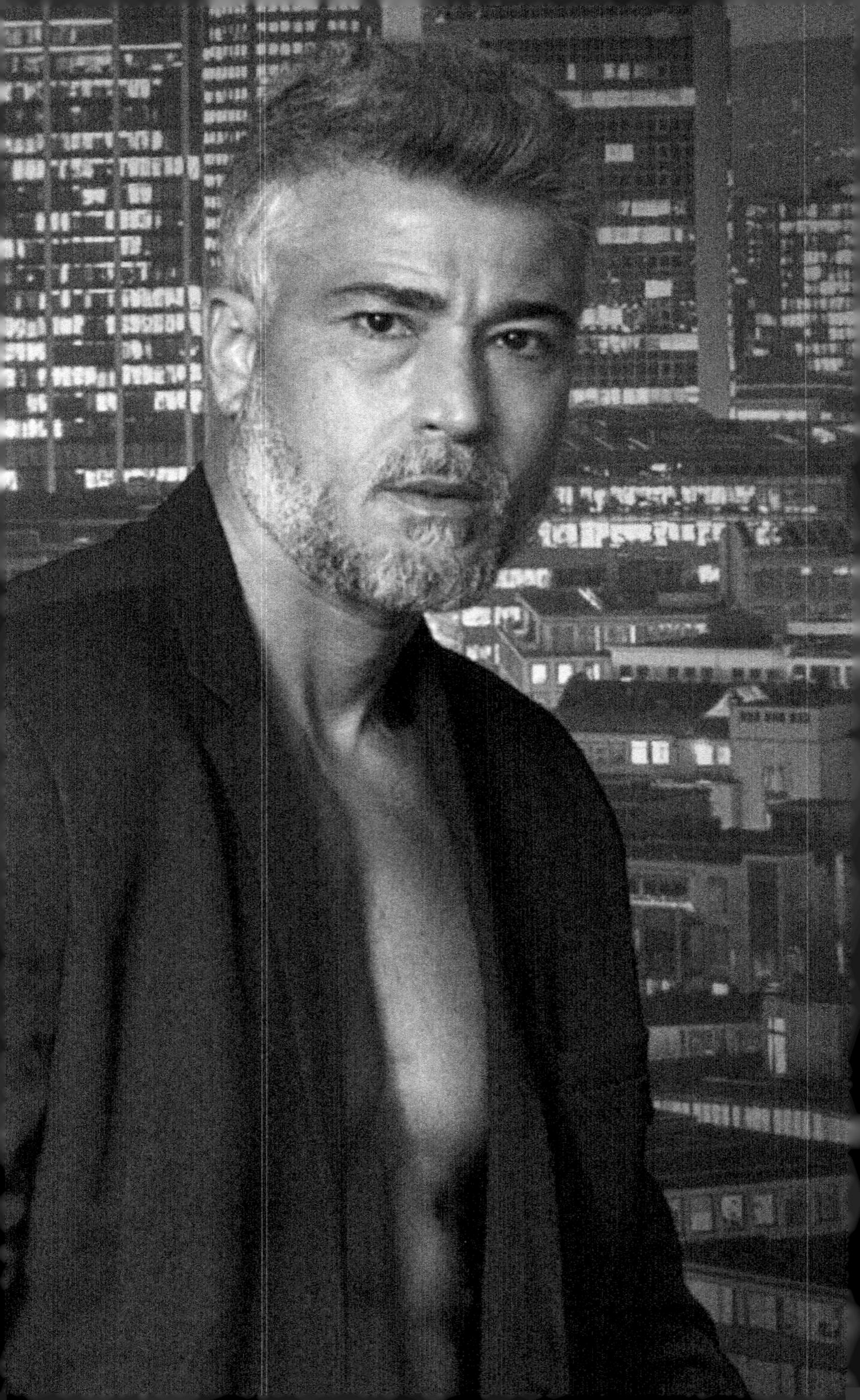

CHAPTER
EIGHT
BELLE

O h, man. I'm suffering from orgasm overload that might lead to a lifelong addiction. Actually, I'm pretty sure I'm already addicted to Dante Arakas. The surly mob boss stole my freaking heart the first night we met, and I have no hope of ever getting it back.

"Are you ready to head to work?" Aaron, one of my new permanent bodyguards, knocks on the door.

"Motherfucker," Dante growls against my lips as I smile. "I hate you leaving me all alone three nights a week," he grumbles for the millionth time since I moved in two months ago. We've had this same argument so many times, I've lost track.

"You sleep part of the time I'm gone." I attempt to placate him. He started working normal business hours at the club after the poisoning attempt, and most of the family business meetings are held at the compound. I'm trying to switch to day shift so I have more time with him, but I have to wait until a position becomes available.

The construction is mostly finished now except for a few buildings on the edge of the massive property, which is surrounded by a tall privacy fence and several booby traps just in case. I'm slowly getting used to the drastic change my simple life took after meeting and falling for the mafia boss.

"I barely sleep anytime you're not lying next to me." Dante wraps his arms tightly around me and sighs. "But I won't stand in the way of you working because I know your job is important to you."

"Thank you, gramps." I still get a kick out of seeing his dark eyes flash fire when I use the nickname. "I'll see you in the morning." Standing on my tiptoes, I kiss his lips one last time before I grab my bag. "And I'll make up for my absence." I wink before blowing him a kiss.

"And your sharp tongue," he calls after me.

"With my sharp tongue." I laugh and follow my bodyguards out.

Work is insane. Multiple trauma victims come rolling in the door at the same time, and I end up running from room to room all night long. Needless to say, I'm dead on my feet when my morning replacement comes strolling in.

After the busy night, I barely have the strength to change from my hospital scrubs into my street clothes, but I decide to take a quick shower in the doctor's lounge to wash all the grime from the busy day off me. "I'll be right back," I tell my two bodyguards and leave them sitting on the sofa watching morning talk shows.

I turn the water to stinging hot and step under the spray as the lights go out. My heart stumbles as I realize something isn't right. A hand comes out of nowhere and wraps around my mouth and pulls me out of the shower. I automatically react, digging my teeth into the smelly hand pinching my nose closed. I kick out at the unknown person attempting to drag me to the door.

"Stop or I'll break your goddamn neck," my assailant hisses when my foot makes contact with his leg. A horrible pain bursts through the back of my head as everything goes dark.

I blink awake, lying on dirty carpet in the back of a van with my hands behind my back. When I attempt to sit up, I realize there are plastic bands wrapped around my wrists and ankles and a stinky rag tied around my mouth. Turning off my intense fear, I wiggle each of my limbs to check for injuries. The back of my head throbs, but I can't feel any other signs of harm. Oh, fudge-muffin. Dante is going to flip the hell out when he finds out I'm gone.

The van comes to a stop, interrupting my thoughts, and I suddenly realize I have greater immediate problems. My kidnapper is going to realize I'm awake when he comes back here.

Closing my eyes, I lie still, hoping to fool the jerk. I hear the vehicle door creak open, and the soon-to-be-dead criminal grumbles something to someone else. Oh great. There are two of them.

Brightness hits my closed eyelids as the door opens, but I force myself to stay still. "Why is she unconscious?"

I recognize that voice flashes through my mind seconds before all hell breaks loose. Dante's men come from all sides and attack the two men standing at the back of the van. I roll out and drop to the ground as the sounds of flesh hitting flesh followed by loud grunts fill the air around me. I somehow manage to wiggle under the van, even though my hands and feet are still tied snuggly with the plastic bands.

Closing my eyes, I ask the universe to let me survive long enough to call Dante gramps again. I lose track of time while my heart nearly beats out of my chest. "Dr. Girardi." Taking a deep breath, I open my eyes and see Carlton crawling under the van to take hold of my arms. "Let me help you out." After pulling me out from under the vehicle, he cuts the plastic cuffs off of my hands and feet before lifting me against his chest.

As he rushes over toward the black SUV that just pulled up, I glance over his shoulder and get my first look at the desolate land around me. Ick. Trash and broken-down cars litter the vast property as far as the eye can see. Over on one side, there's a little white shack. Well, I assume it used to be white at some point. Right now, the paint is peeling in so many spots, the building is mostly just rotted wood.

Several men lay sprawled across the unkempt yard while another group, all men I recognize from Dante's organization, mill around. I'm pretty sure they're looking for survivors. Before I'm able to think too hard about the situation, I tell myself to turn on my blinders and concentrate on getting back to Dante. I've already decided I want to be a part of his life, even if it means turning a blind eye to the unsavory part of his world.

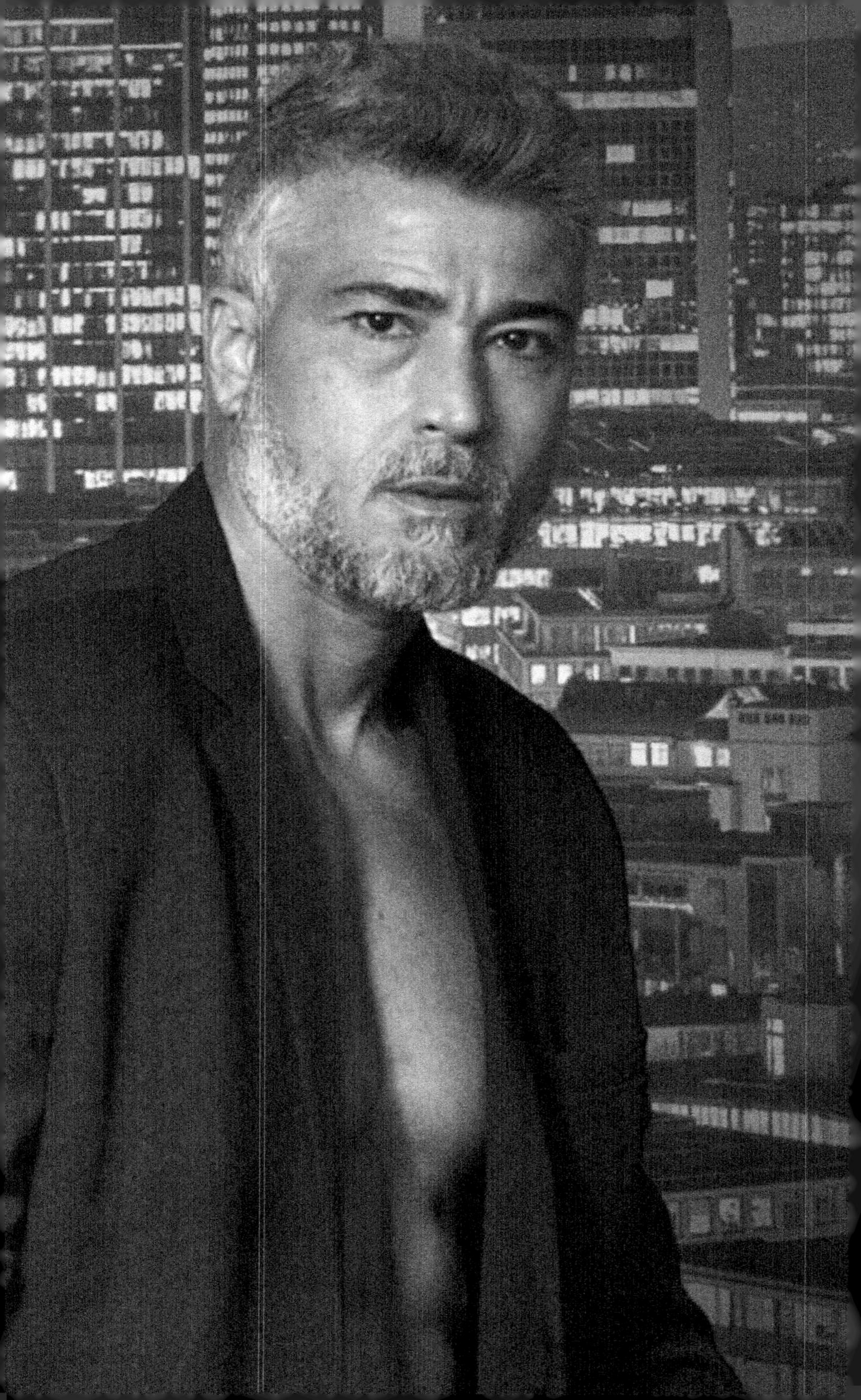

CHAPTER NINE

DANTE

I spend all morning feeling an unfamiliar tightness in my chest. I'm not sure what's causing this sensation, but I instinctively know not to ignore it. When our daily security meeting comes to an end, Bruno rushes over. "You need to see this."

He holds out his cell phone, and I take the device as dread slams into me. I glance down at the screen and look down at the message. *What the fuck am I reading?*

"Aaron and Logan were found dead in the hospital break room." Motherfucker. I want to throw up as I read the information on the screen. This shit can't be happening. My little beauty's security detail is dead. Fear like I've never known cuts through me.

"Tell me she's alive," I beg as pain lances my body.

"Carlton and his crew are on the way to the hospital now." Dmitri places his hand on my back. "Don't worry. We'll get her back." I know we fucking will. There isn't any other choice. I can't live without my little beauty.

"I want her fucking found." My roar echoes around the bar. Needing to maintain control, I push my emotions to the back of my mind and concentrate on fixing this situation. Once I'm sure my little beauty is safe, I can take care of business.

Whoever dared to touch Belle better find a big goddamn rock to hide under. Because I'm going to find him. And when I do, he's going to die a painful fucking death.

"I think we have something." Bruno rushes over and signals for us to follow him.

Dmitri and I follow him to the car idling in front of my house. "One of the cameras across the street from the hospital caught the license plate on the van her kidnapper used," Bruno explains as we speed away from Silver Spoon Falls. "One of our friends in the FBI was able to get the manufacturer to trace its location using the onboard computer. The coordinates just came through."

"Do you have eyes on her?" I need to know she's okay.

"Not yet, but Carlton and Elliot are almost there." Both of my men have been loyal to me and this organization for years. I have no doubt they'll do whatever it takes to save my little beauty.

Uncomfortable silence fills the vehicle during the longest ride of my life. All I can think of is getting Belle back in my arms in one piece. Then I'm going to kill the piece of shit who did this, and I'm never letting my little beauty out of my sight again.

"Don't worry." Dmitri looks over at me and attempts to soothe my raging emotions. "We'll get her back."

"I know," I growl, knowing there's no other choice for me. I can't imagine trying to live without her. "And I'm going to kill the dumb fuck who dared to touch my woman."

"Mother..." Bruno stares at his phone for several seconds before glancing up. "You aren't going to believe who has her."

I grab his phone and stare at the message as shock rolls through me. This is more than personal. This is war. Leandro fucking Barone has no idea the shit he just stepped in. He approached us months ago, asking for help with his bar after the locals decided to run him and the new strip club out of town. He was on the verge of bankruptcy and offered us ownership stake in the bar in exchange for enough money to get his ass out of trouble. I only considered taking the deal because the bar makes the perfect location to run my organization discreetly.

Once the sale went through and we made peace with the town, the asshole decided he wasn't happy with the terms of the transaction. I told him to fuck off since I'd kept my end of the bargain and he got rich off the sale. I knew Leandro was disgruntled, but I had no idea he was a fucking idiot.

The pictures on Bruno's phone tell a different story. It's easy to put two and two together and come up with a snake who decided to stab me in the back by joining forces with my cartel enemies. That's a mistake you only make once, which this dumb son-of-a-bitch is about to find out.

We drive up to what looks like an abandoned junkyard. "Just as we've been suspecting, the Carmona Kings have been using this place to hide out near Silver Spoon Falls," Bruno informs me. We've been keeping an eye on all large available or abandoned properties near town, knowing the Kings would need someplace close to stay off the radar. This place came to our attention recently, and we've been watching it closely.

"When the van headed this way, we figured they were heading to this property," Bruno tells me.

Dmitri cuts in, "I split up the crew and sent half here and kept half at the compound to make sure this isn't a diversion for their real attack." I appreciate my nephew's effort to take control while my mind has been elsewhere. He's proven that my unwavering trust isn't misplaced.

I forget all about the goddamn cartel and my soon-to-be former business partner when I see Carlton carrying my girl toward the SUV. Ignoring the threat of danger, I hop out and rush over to them. "Are you okay?" I grab Belle from my man's arms and pull her sweet body against mine. I'm able to take a deep breath for the first time since I found out she'd been taken. In that moment, I promise myself that no one will ever get close enough to my girl to hurt her again.

"I'm fine." My little beauty lays her head against my shoulder and twists her hands in the front of my shirt. "I'm so freaking glad to see you."

"I'm not ever going to let you out of my sight again." I hop back in the SUV with her in my arms, just in case my men haven't rounded up all the stragglers. "You aren't allowed to give me a scare like this ever the fuck again or I'll spank your luscious ass red."

"First, I'd like to point out that this was not my fault." She stares into my eyes and smirks. "And second, you threatening to spank me isn't really a threat at all."

"Keep it up," I warn her as my cock hardens and pokes into her luscious ass. "And my men will get more than they bargained for when they watch me spank your ass."

"Oh. Kinky," Belle jokes and snuggles against me. "You really keep me on my toes."

I didn't want to do this in front of my nephew and our men, but I can't stop myself from kissing her soft lips and stating. "I fucking love you." I've been waiting for the right moment to tell her how I feel, and this is it. "I can't stand the thought of living the rest of my life without you by my side." I push Belle's messy hair behind her ears and stare into her honey eyes. She's the most beautiful sight I've ever seen. Her eyes fill with tears, and I rub my thumbs across her soft skin to wipe them away when those tears trail down her cheeks.

"I love you, too. Gramps." She laughs. "And I can't imagine my life without you, either." Her words soothe my soul, and relief flows through me when I realize today's events haven't convinced my brave little beauty to run from me.

"As soon as I can arrange it, I'm going to marry you." No use asking since there's no way I'd let Belle tell me no. I'd just find a way to convince her. "Then I'm going to knock your little ass up until we're too old to have any more kids. You'll be too busy chasing our kids around to give me gray hairs."

"I wouldn't count on your plan working, gramps. I'm sure I'll find the time to give you gray hairs while I keep up with the kids. And my job," she throws in, and I realize there's no way I can ask her to give up her career. But I will ensure that she's perfectly safe any time she's away from me.

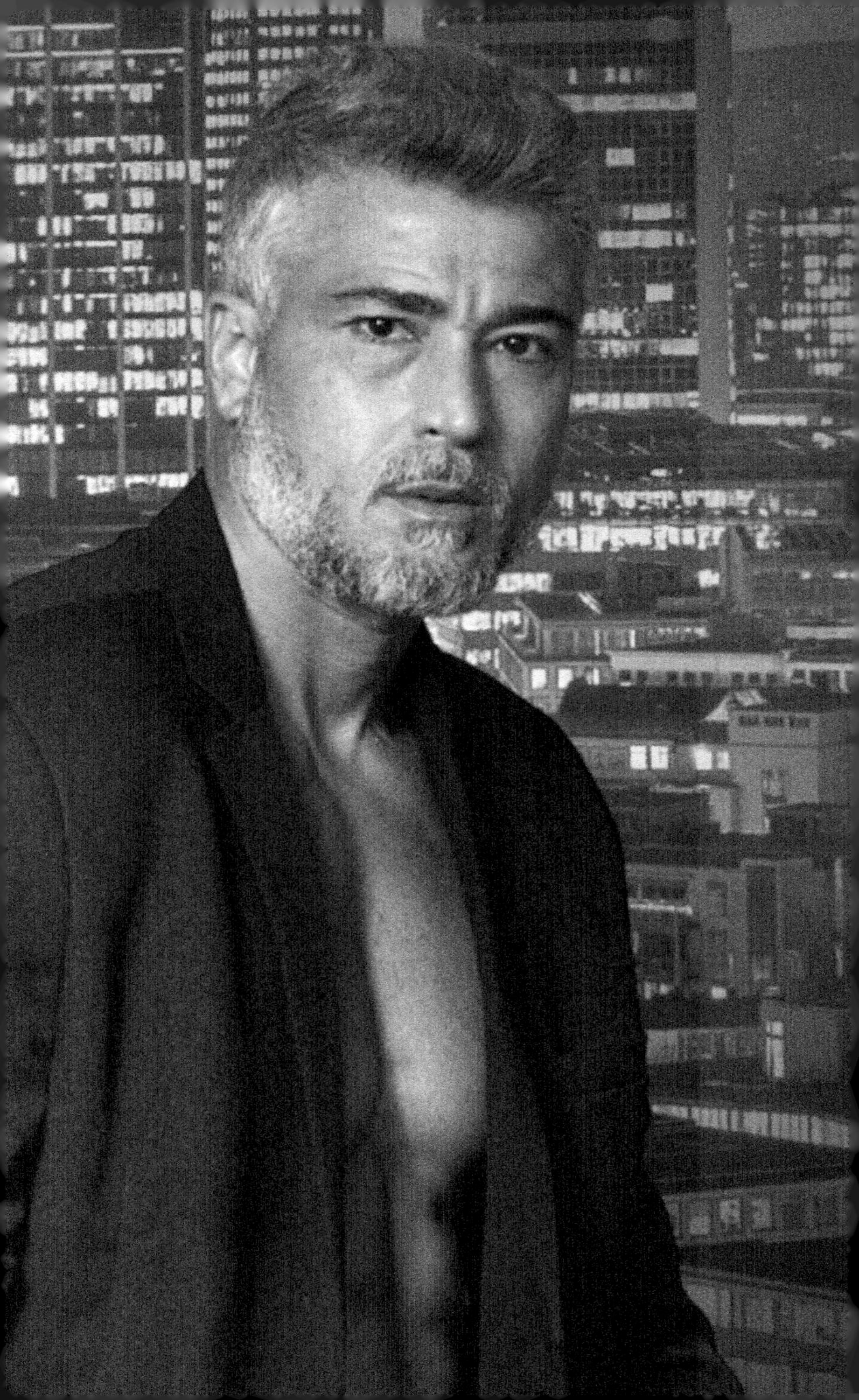

EPILOGUE ONE
BELLE

Once Dante Arakas makes up his mind, things happen at warp speed. Two weeks and three days after my kidnapping, we have a quick wedding ceremony in the Silver Spoon Falls courthouse. Dante wanted to have a huge, fancy affair, but I talked him into toning things down. After all the excitement of the last few weeks, I wanted something small and private.

Now, we're on our way to a private Caribbean island for our dream honeymoon. What can I say? He spoils me rotten.

I relax and lay my head on Dante's shoulder as the private plane levels off. "You spoil me rotten."

The massive diamond ring he slipped on my finger a few hours ago sparkles in the sunlight as he brings my hand to his lips for a kiss. "I'd do anything to make you happy. I love you more than anything in the world."

"You know what would make me happy right now?" I reach down and run my hand over the front of my husband's dress pants, feeling his cock hardening under my touch.

"I love the way you think, Dr. Arakas." Dante kisses the side of my neck before pressing the button on his seat to tell the flight attendant and his men that we're going to rest in the small bedroom. Knowing they realize he really means we're about to get our honeymoon started in the back of the plane doesn't embarrass me in the least.

As I follow Dante to the back of the plane, I forget about everyone else as my handsome husband commands all of my attention.

When he shuts the door behind us and points at the bed, I feel my pulse accelerate. "Strip or I'll end up ripping that dress off your gorgeous body." My husband's caveman approach really works for me.

While I quickly remove my wedding clothes, I watch Dante slip off his tie and unbutton his dress shirt. He drops them on the floor at his feet before giving his pants the same treatment. Once I'm naked, I lay back on the bed and wait for him to prowl over to me. I think my husband needs a little motivation to hurry up, so I slide my finger through the wetness dripping from my center and whimper, "I need you. Now."

"You don't have to ask me twice," Dante groans and drops to his knees next to the small bed.

He takes his time pulling me to the edge of the bed before running his tongue frustratingly slowly up the inside of my thigh, and I grumble, "Hurry up, gramps." I'm not in the mood for slow. Right now, I want my powerful mob boss to ravish me.

Dante stares into my eyes while biting down gently on the sensitive skin of my inner thigh. "Perfection cannot be rushed, little beauty."

"Who said?" I really need him to get a move on before I self-combust.

"Me," he insists. My eyes cross as my head falls back against the soft covers when he sucks my clit between his lips and lightly bites down before pressing his tongue deep into my wet center. I arch my back and wrap my leg around his back, trying to motivate him to get a move on. My begging finally works, and Dante loses control. He devours me with his teeth and tongue while his fingers press deep into my pussy.

Mr. Overachiever Mob Boss insists on giving me three mind-blowing orgasms before he's done using his lips, teeth, and tongue on me. I'm limp from pleasure by the time Dante kisses his way up the center of my body.

"I love you to the moon and back," he whispers against the side of my neck before sucking the tender skin against his teeth, marking me.

"I love you, too," I croak out and realize my throat is scratchy from all the screaming I've been doing since my husband decided to join the mile-high club with me. I forget about my embarrassment when he finally lines his cock up with my entrance and thrusts forward.

Digging my nails into his shoulders, I hold on for the wild ride. When he circles his hips while rubbing my clit, an unexpected orgasm blasts through me, and I scream again as my husband comes shouting my name.

Dante rolls over and pulls me against his side as our breathing slows. The two of us barely fit on the small bed, but we make it work.

I place my chin on his chest and smile into his eyes. "So, were you serious when you said you want a house full of kids?"

"I plan to knock you up before we return to Silver Spoon Falls." He runs his hand through my hair and pulls me close for a kiss.

I bite down gently on his bottom lip. "Too late."

Dante sits up suddenly and pulls me into his lap. "What?" I think I finally managed to shock my mob boss husband.

"Let me explain things to you." I run my finger down the center of this masculine chest. "When a man uses this." I squeeze his cock and feel it begin to harden in my grasp. "Here." I take his hand and place it against my wet opening. "Without birth control." I smile up at him. "A baby forms inside here." I hold his hand against my belly.

He opens his mouth and closes it a few times without any words emerging. Holy cow. My usually vocal husband is speechless. And I'm pretty sure he's blinking away tears.

"I don't deserve you." He hugs me close and runs his nose against the side of my neck. "But I'm keeping you anyway."

"You're keeping us." I smile up at him before snuggling into his warm embrace. Somehow, I managed to tame the King of the Texas Underworld. And he's made me his queen. Life doesn't get any better than this.

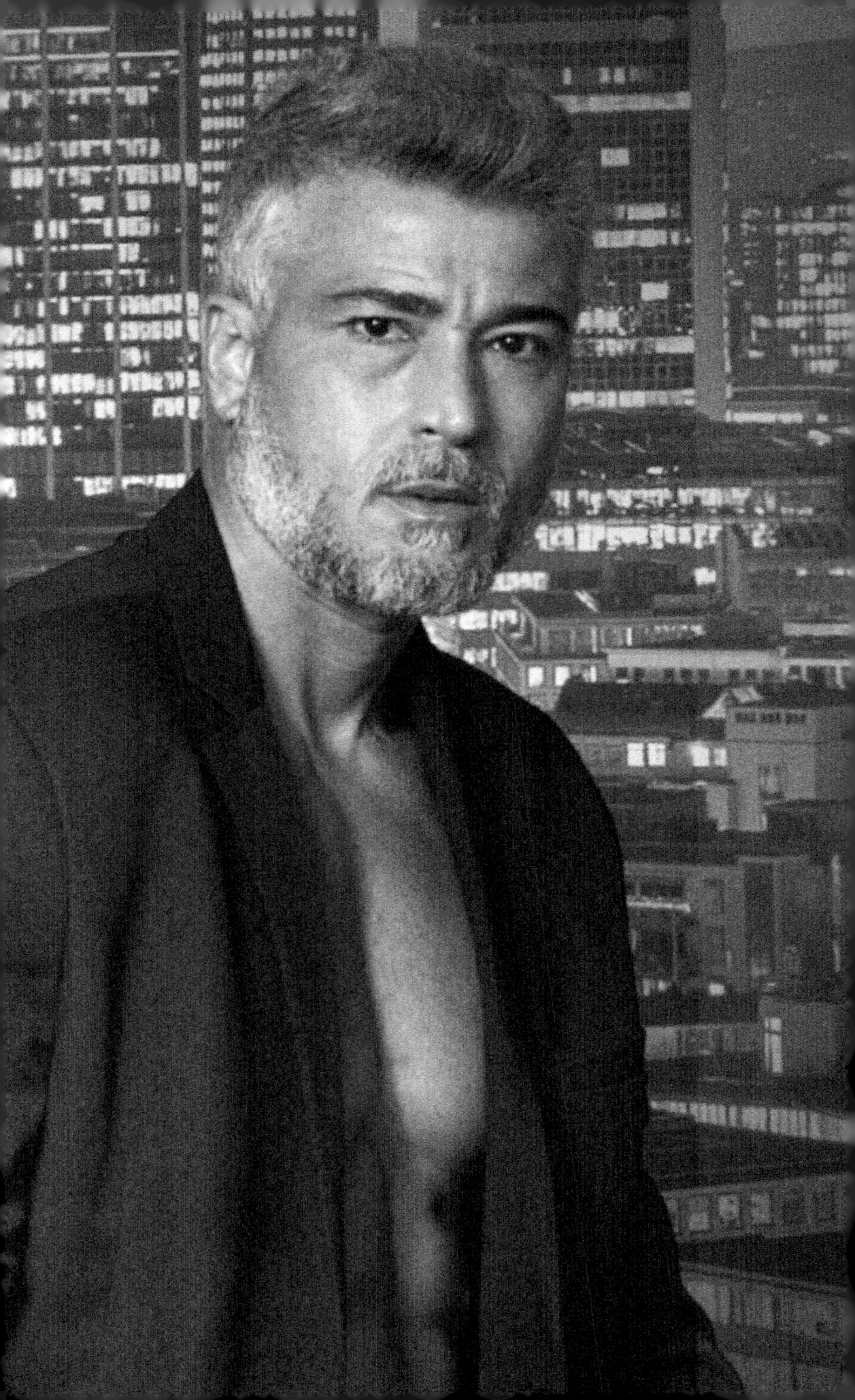

EPILOGUE TWO
DANTE

FOUR YEARS LATER

Most men give their wives jewelry or a new car for a wedding present, but I'm not most men. I wanted to make sure my wife could continue her career without any threat to her safety, so I gave her an urgent care clinic for her wedding present. It might've been a little excessive, but I'll do whatever it takes to make sure my family is safe. I breathe easier knowing my men are controlling the security at the urgent care. Their number one job is making sure my wife is safe at all times. I personally designed the urgent care security system and I can guarantee the president doesn't have more protection than Belle.

Over the last four years, we've found a way to make our lives as "normal" as possible. My wife didn't want our children raised by outsiders, so we skipped hiring a nanny. The first few months of parenthood were trying until we figured out a way to make everything work. Of course, my beautiful wife makes it all look easy.

Belle works two days a week at the Silver Spoon Falls Urgent Care and spends the rest of the time at home with us. To keep the urgent care running in her absence, we hired four outstanding local doctors to work the other five days of the week.

I've been slowly handing over more control to my nephew, and Dmitri is thriving with the extra responsibilities. He's almost ready for me to step back and let him assume control of the organization. I will always keep an eye on things, but I trust

Dmitri and Bruno to keep everything running smoothly. We're still working to get rid of the cartels, but the fuckers are like cockroaches. As soon as we get rid of one, another two pop up to cause trouble.

Our close proximity to the border and Houston makes us a continuous target to the bastards, but they're starting to realize I won't go down without a fight. And so far, they're losing the fight big time.

We take turns making sure the little monsters stay out of trouble while maintaining both our busy positions, and today is my day to supervise the hellions.

While all is quiet, I'm sitting at the desk in my home office reading an email when my three-year-old son comes blasting into the room. "Daddy!" This kid only has one volume—earsplitting. We've been working on teaching him to moderate his voice. Unsuccessfully so far.

"Dmitri." I attempt to give my son my sternest look, but it has little effect on my mini-me. "What did I tell you about running around the house screaming for no reason?"

"But Daddy!" My son is a professional at arguing. "I have a reason," he insists. "Marissa's eating Rover's treats." Holy fucking hell.

I rush around the desk and take off running down the hallway. My wife is going to have a stroke when she gets home if she finds out our two-year-old daughter ate dog treats while I was in charge of watching the kids.

"I don't wanna die!" My daughter's wail fills the hallway as I meet Bruno at the kitchen door. We find my daughter lying on the kitchen floor, wailing at the top of her lungs. "I don't wanna die."

"Marissa." I shove Bruno out of the way and lift my daughter against my chest. "What's wrong?"

"Daddy." I wince as her loud screech assaults my eardrums. "I don't want to die."

I gently search her tiny body for any signs of injury and breathe a sigh of relief when I find she doesn't appear to be harmed. "Why do you think you're going to die?"

I sit her down on the edge of the countertop, attempting to calm her down enough to find out what the hell is going on.

"Meetwee dared me to eat Rovo's tweats." Now, I know part of the story. I glare at my suddenly guilty-looking son over Marissa's head. "He said they's poison, and now I'm gonna die." Her voice gets louder with each word until I'm pretty sure my ears are bleeding from the damage. "I don't wanna die."

Her pitiful pout causes my heart to clench while I debate how to handle this situation. I should let her continue believing the bullshit her brother fed her, but seeing my tiny little girl so upset breaks my fucking heart. Parenthood is much fucking harder than running a goddamn organized crime family.

"You're not going to die, sweetheart," I tell Marissa and watch as she instantly perks up and her wails come to an abrupt halt.

Bruno's face turns red while my friend tries to hold back his laughter, and I discreetly flip the asshole off behind my daughter's back before telling Marissa, "But you're going to spend a while in time-out for letting your brother talk you into doing something you know is wrong.

"And you." I glare at Dmitri, searching my brain for the appropriate punishment for his crime. "Are going to spend the afternoon cleaning your room to make up for being mean to your sister."

When my son opens his mouth to argue, I glare at him, daring the little shit to try me. "Yes, Daddy." Dmitri sighs, finally realizing how easy I'm letting him off.

"Well played," Bruno compliments me after we send the children to their rooms for their punishments. "Your wife has done a great job training you."

"That she has," I agree. After all, you can't argue with the truth.

Later that night, my wife snuggles against my side and runs her hand across my chest. "I heard the kids gave you a busy afternoon." I should've known she'd find out. Nothing stays secret in this house.

"They did." I smile at Belle, feeling her luscious curves pressed against my side. Her sweet body is tempting me to forget how tired I am. "How did you know?" I have to ask.

"I knew Dmitri did something when I saw how clean his room is," Belle explains. "It didn't take much to get him to admit to his crimes."

"Your interrogation skills are top-notch." I laugh and pull her close.

"What can I say?" My wife leans up to kiss my lips. "I learned from the king."

"And your king has a lot more to teach you," I promise as happiness flows through me.

"Promises, promises," Belle whispers against my lips before I spin her around and proceed to show her a few new things. Hopefully, our *new things* will lead to another little monster running around the house.

Coming to Silver Spoon Falls was the best thing I ever did. I somehow got lucky enough to find the perfect soulmate, partner, and wife. Life couldn't get any better.

THE END OF Belle's KING

Thank you so much for reading Belle's King! I hope you enjoyed the story and will consider leaving a review.

If you'd like to read other books in the Silver Spoon Underworld series, you can find them here: mybook.to/SilverSpoonUnderworld

JOIN MY READER'S GROUP

FIND OUT ABOUT MY NEW RELEASES, SALES AND OTHER PROMOTIONS.

Facebook Group (Hot Heroes and Happy Endings)

Subscribe to My Newsletter

GET HOW TO LOVE A HEARTBREAKER WHEN YOU SUBSCRIBE TO MY NEWSLETTER

Loni Ree Romance Newsletter

ALSO BY LONI REE

Find all my books on my website:

https://www.hotheroesandhea.com/

SILVER SPOON MC

The CEO

The Cowboy

The Rockstar

The Architect

The Prince

SILVER SPOON FALLS

Fischer's Catch

Adam's Fugitive

MONSTERS & CURVES

Mr. Nice Guy

First Bite

CELESTIAL FALLS

Cupcakes & Brimstone

Honey & Growls

Hexes & Howls

Whiskers & Wings

Glitz & Growls

Defying Roderick (Related to Celestial Falls)

CURVY CUTIES

Jenna

Emery

BOSS FROM HELL

Over It

Into It

WILD ACES

Spade's Queen

Barrett's Play

Snow's Spell (connected characters)

MEN OF VALOR MC

First Ride

FIELDING-STONE SERIES

Blindsiding Mr. Quinlan

Shocking Mr. Stone

Fielding-Stone Series Boxset

LOVE AT FIRST SIGHT SERIES

Professor Maxwell

Packaged Love

Nerd Boy

Cover Model

Love at First Sight: A Four Book Collection

STANDALONE BOOKS

Hungry For Red (A Salem Experiment Book One)

Finding His Forever (Finding His Love Book One)

Wicked Ways (Hunky Halloween)

Falling for my Enemy

Leaping into Love (Taking the Leap Book 7)

Warm Kisses (Warming Up to Love Book 6)

FOR HER

Keeping Liberty (American Heroes Book Two) (For Her Book 1)

Ignoring the Rules (For Her Book 2)

THE MACKENZIE FAMILY INCLUDES:

KANES' KISSES SERIES

Holly Kisses

Surprise Kisses (Forever Safe Christmas Book 19)

Candy Kisses

Kane's Kisses: A Four Book Collection Boxset

Forever Kisses

SWEET BEGINNINGS

Sweet Treat

Sugar Pie

LOVING A BENNETT BOY

Mr. CEO Jerk

Mr. Director Sir

Mr. Boss Man

SPARKS IN JUNIPER

Ignite My Heart

FINDING MS. RIGHT

Claiming Ms. Off Limits

Roping Ms. Imposter

PLAYING RIORDAN

Catching Payton

Scoring Gina

FALLING HARD AND FAST

Can't Resist Her

THE MERGER

Blake's Fall

Lukas' Love

Drew's Fight

FIRSTS SERIES

First Sight

First Touch

SWEET ON YOU (CLEAN, SWEET ROMANCE) Writing as L. Ree

Knox's Surprise (Sweet on You Book 1)

Trace's Fire (Sweet on You Book 2)

Jordan's Gift (Sweet on You Book 3)

Jason's Luck (Sweet on You Book 4)

About the Author

USA Today **Bestselling Author**

Loni Ree is a very busy mom of six who loves to read, and she finds that it helps her escape the chaos of everyday life. She likes quick reads that are red-hot and on the excessive side. Writing has also been a passion of hers, and Loni decided to share the stories floating around in her mind. Her short, steamy stories are a little over the top because she believes reading should be an escape from real life. She writes about hot heroes finding their beautiful soulmates and fighting for their happy endings!

Loni also has an alternate pen name L. Ree. If you like clean, sweet romance, check out her L. Ree books.

Website: Hotheroesandhea.com
https://linktr.ee/loniree19

- facebook.com/lonireeromance
- twitter.com/loni_ree
- instagram.com/lonireeromance
- amazon.com/author/loniree
- bookbub.com/authors/loni-ree
- goodreads.com/LoniRee
- pinterest.com/loni01013104

Printed in Great Britain
by Amazon